PHOBOS

CUPID'S CAPTIVE, BOOK TWO

Eva Pohler

Eva Pohler Books
20011 Park Ranch
San Antonio, Texas 78259
www.evapohler.com

Publisher's Note: This is a work of fiction. Names, characters, places, and incidents are a product of the author's imagination. Locales and public names are sometimes used for atmospheric purposes. Any resemblance to actual people, living or dead, or to businesses, companies, events, institutions, or locales is completely coincidental.

Book Layout ©2017 BookDesignTemplates.com

Book Cover Design by Keri Knutson

Phobos/ Eva Pohler. -- 1st ed.
Paperback ISBN: 978-1-958390-62-7

"I guess we finally know who the superior twin is, don't we?"—PHOBOS

"I believe we've always known that, brother,"--DEIMOS.

Contents

For my husband.

The Shack

I don't know what Artemis was thinking, sending us here with flannel shirts," Deimos complained inside the dilapidated shack they would call home for the next six months. "It's too damn hot."

Phobos had already stripped his off, preferring to go without a shirt altogether than to spend one more miserable second wearing what felt like a wet blanket. "Preach, brother."

Cupid dug through the bag Artemis had given each of them. "Thank the gods, there's a clean t-shirt in here." He whipped off the flannel and pulled on the white t-shirt, grinning with relief.

Deimos followed suit. "Amen, brother. This is much better."

Cupid's brows flew up. "So, you *have* forgiven me?"

"We're going to be trapped here together for six months," Deimos said. "I'd rather not make it worse."

"What about you, Phobos?" Cupid asked as he folded the flannel shirt and returned it to the bag.

"Give me time."

Cupid frowned and nodded. "Of course."

Phobos noticed Ellie standing in the corner, enjoying the show.

He crossed the room and glared down at her. "What are you looking at?"

Her eyes roamed across his bare chest before she met his gaze. "I'm going to the well to wash my bedding. Would you like me to wash yours, too?"

"I don't want you anywhere near my bedding," Phobos said.

He could tell by her expression that his words had stung. Good.

She stepped back and turned to his brothers. "Deimos? Cupid? Can I wash your bedding?"

"Thanks, Ellie," Cupid said. "That's very kind of you."

"I'm good," Deimos said without looking at her.

Phobos groaned when Cupid followed Ellie to their room, offering to help her. He wondered who would take the top bunk and who the bottom. Phobos had already called dibs on the bottom bunk in the five-by-seven-foot "bedroom" he shared with Deimos. To Phobos, "closet" seemed like a better word. Even the closet in his London flat was bigger.

The entire shack was no more than twelve feet by twelve feet.

He supposed being stuck with Ellie and his brothers in the Texas heat in a falling-down shack without indoor plumbing or electricity was better than being condemned to the Titan Pit.

But not by much.

Because he was accustomed to sensing people—both gods and mortals—before they announced themselves, he was startled by a knock at the door. His lack of powers was unnerving. This was going to be an agonizingly long six months.

They'd left the door ajar, because of the heat, and the person knocking there was fully visible. It was a young woman carrying a deep plastic tub, a broom, and a lantern. She had long brown hair pulled back from her face with a clip. Her brown eyes were round and lined with dark, thick lashes. Her brows were thick, too, which Phobos found sexy. She was smiling up at him. Maybe things weren't going to be so bad here, after all.

"Hi," she said. "I'm Jaquelyn. My parents told me to bring you these."

"Come in," Phobos said.

She was wearing denim cut-offs and a t-shirt with the letters YOLO printed on it. By his estimation, she looked to be about seventeen.

Jaquelyn set the tub down on the rickety old table on one side of the room. "I have some canteens for each of you. It's important to stay hydrated."

"It's ridiculously hot here," Deimos said. "I'm sure those will come in handy."

"Yeah, August is the worst," Jaquelyn said. "Plan to swim every day to keep from dying of heatstroke."

Phobos lifted his brows. "That sounds nice. I saw a big pond on the way in."

"My parents would rather you not swim there," Jaquelyn said as her cheeks turned pink.

"Then where?" Phobos asked, already missing his spa on Mount Olympus.

"In the streams. Just watch out for Rusty, our bull, if you swim in the northeast pasture. He shouldn't bother you but be aware that he's there."

"Got it," Deimos said. "And where is the northeast pasture from here?"

"My dad's coming by in about an hour to give you a tour. He wanted me to bring this stuff down, so you could get settled first."

Deimos offered Jaquelyn his hand. "I'm Deimos. It's nice to meet you, Jaquelyn."

She shook it. "Likewise."

Phobos offered his. "Phobos."

Cupid entered with a bundle of bedding in his arms, followed by Ellie.

"Hi," Cupid said. "I'm Cupid, and this is Ellie."

"Hello," Ellie said.

"Hi." Jaquelyn gave her a smile. "I've seen you before, on television. Aren't you a pitcher for the Seminoles?"

Ellie blushed. "I was. A lot has happened since then."

"But it's only been two months since you won the world series," Jaquelyn pointed out.

"Do you play?" Ellie asked.

"I wish. I used to, but not anymore."

"That's too bad," Ellie said.

Jaquelyn averted her eyes. "I was just telling Phobos and Deimos that my dad will be down to give you a tour of the ranch in about an hour. My parents sent this tub of things to help you get settled. There's a toolbox in here from my dad. And my mom sent some cleaning supplies and rags, if you want to wipe this place down."

"Oh, good," Ellie said. "And you brought a broom. The floors could use a good sweeping."

"Yeah," Jaquelyn said. "No one's used this place in a few years."

Phobos fought the urge to say it looked like it hadn't been used in a few *decades*.

"I've also brought a box of laundry detergent, bars of soap, two bottles of shampoo, and four clean towels," Jaquelyn added. "And I guess you saw the well on your way over. You can use it for drinking and for clean water to wash yourselves and your clothes and bedding. That's what this big tub is for—for washing and rinsing. Just be sure to dump the soapy water away from the animals."

"Thank you," Phobos said. He'd never had to launder a thing in his life, but he reminded himself that there were worse fates.

"You're welcome to use the clothesline across from the well to dry your things. We have a washer and dryer and rarely use the clothesline anymore."

"Thanks," Cupid said.

"So, you want us to bathe at the well?" Ellie asked.

Jaquelyn's cheeks turned pink again. "Only when you want to use soap and shampoo. We'd rather you not use chemicals in the streams, since the animals drink from it."

Phobos could tell that Ellie wasn't happy about that.

"Oh, and there's an outhouse under the tree over there—I'm not sure if you saw it. It's for when you need to go at night. I brought you a flashlight, so you can find your way in the dark. You're welcome to use the restroom in the main house during the day."

"That's great news," Ellie said. "What a relief!"

Jaqueline laughed. "Hopefully, you won't have to use the outhouse at all."

"Especially if you avoid drinking at night," Cupid said.

"Which shouldn't be hard," Jaquelyn added with a laugh. "You'll be ready to crash after supper. Trust me."

Phobos had normally gone at least three days without sleep, but he'd also never had his powers stripped from him. Now that he thought about it, he could use a nap.

"Just in case you want to read or hang out before bed, here's a lantern," Jaqueline said.

"Awesome. Thanks," Cupid said.

"We have breakfast at six, lunch at noon, and supper at eight. Mom told me to tell you she's planning on feeding you this evening."

"We look forward to it," Deimos said.

"Well, it was nice meeting you all." Jaquelyn turned to the door. "I'm sorry we don't have a nicer place for you to stay in."

Phobos noticed her glance at his bare chest. He'd been hoping she would. He'd begun to believe she was more interested in Ellie than in him or his brothers, but that glance, and her awkward smile when she knew she was caught, had told him otherwise.

"Thank you," Phobos said. "I suppose we'll be seeing a lot of each other."

"Yep. See you."

Phobos watched her walk away, past the well, and back to the main house. Cupid followed with his bundle of bedding. Ellie emptied the tub of everything but the laundry detergent and used it to carry her bedding as she followed Cupid to the well. Phobos was surprised when Ellie didn't look back at him. As much as he despised her, he'd taken a sick kind of pleasure in watching her long for him. His heart could feel both arrows compelling him to hate and to love, but the hate won out. Had Ellie given up already?

"I saw the way you were looking at Jaquelyn," Deimos said, bringing Phobos from his thoughts.

"So?"

"Try not to make things worse."

"Worse?" Phobos scoffed. "How could they possibly get worse? I'd say a pretty girl makes things better."

"Like it did with Ellie?" Deimos snapped.

"That was different."

"You could still break her heart."

"Ellie's? Why should I care? Do you?"

"Jaquelyn's."

Phobos dug through the bag from Artemis and found a white t-shirt. He didn't want to hurt the mortal, but he needed something to lift him from this misery. The hate he felt for Ellie was overwhelming. Every time he looked at her, he wanted to slap her, crush her, hurt her. He knew it was the arrow of hate that was driving his hatred, but it was powerful and all-consuming, no matter how much he tried to reason with himself.

Even when he focused on the memories that he'd made with her—of kissing her mouth and throat in Selene's cave, of touching her breasts in Cupid's swimming pool, of kneading her between the legs on Circe's island—they only further fueled his hatred. The only thing that made him feel better was knowing that she ached for him and couldn't have him.

Cupid pumped water into the plastic tub while Ellie added some detergent. Then they sat on the stone ledge around the pump with the tub between them and scrubbed the bedding.

Ellie looked around, finding the place wasn't as bad as she had originally thought. The farmhouse was prettier from the back. If the Garcia family were to clean off their front porch, it would make a huge difference, in her opinion. Replacing the rotten siding, missing shutters, and broken window in the front would do wonders as well.

The family kept everything tidy in the back. The dirt driveway that ran in a straight line from the side of the house to the barn divided the area into two sides. The farmhouse, well, clothesline, shack and outhouse were on the west side of it, while the garage, chicken coop, pens, and stables were on the east. Pea gravel covered the ground and most of the driveway.

Everything in the back was utilitarian—nothing fancy. But the front had been beautiful until you reached the front porch and saw the junk in front of the worn-down farmhouse. The dirt road had curved from the main road around a stack of boulders on the left, over a large pond, and past a garden on the right. The road had curved again in front of the house, in a semicircle, before splitting two ways: if you went straight, you would go into the garage. If you turned left, you would drive past the house, the well, and the shack and into the barn.

Ellie imagined what the farmhouse would look like with repairs and fresh paint.

"A penny for your thoughts," Cupid said.

"I was just thinking how pretty this place is, now that the shock of coming here has worn off."

"It's hard to see the beauty when it's so damn hot." Cupid washed his face with some of the water and allowed it to drip down his neck.

"It's the hottest time of the day. Hopefully it'll cool down this evening."

"The shack isn't much, is it," Cupid said without inflection. "Three plain rooms."

"It's certainly not your castle." Ellie laughed.

Cupid laughed, too. "Yeah. It's a little different."

"I doubt we'll be spending much time in it."

"At least it has a lot of windows. I opened them up first thing, to get the air circulating."

"But no screens. I hope we won't get eaten alive by mosquitoes."

"I hadn't thought of that."

"Check out that chicken coop. I wonder if we'll wake up to roosters singing cock-a-doodle-do in the morning."

"Gods, I hope not." Cupid wrung out the excess water from the bedding. "If you'll hold the sheets and blankets, I'll pour out this soapy water and pump in some clean water for rinsing."

Ellie bundled the bedding in her arms while Cupid walked across the gravel and dumped the water near the fence behind the outhouse.

After they'd rinsed the soap out of the bedding, they worked together to hang the sheets, blankets, and pillowcases on the line. They were finishing up when Phobos and Deimos joined them with their bedding rolled up in their arms.

Ellie smiled at them, but Deimos avoided her eyes, and Phobos glared at her.

Without saying a word, she followed Cupid to the shack, where she got to work dusting, wiping up cobwebs, and sweeping all the floors, while Cupid took out each of the mattresses and pillows and beat them against a tree. It hadn't taken long to tidy up the place, because it was so small. Ellie was organizing their supplies in a set of cabinets opposite the table and chairs when the twins returned with Cupid, the plastic tub, and the last of the mattresses.

She'd been hoping they'd remark on the shack's transformation in the short time they'd been out, but after they helped Cupid return the mattress to its bunk, they each sat on one of the four wooden chairs around the table and said nothing. So, after organizing the supplies and putting away the wash bin, Ellie retreated to her and Cupid's room to put the few clothes, toothbrush, and hairbrush Artemis had given her on the shelves in the tiny closet. Then she sat on the bottom bunk, put her hands in her face, and cried.

Phobos stood in the doorway of her room. "What are you blubbering about?"

"What do you think?"

"*You* grew up living in poverty. Think how hard this is for the *rest* of us."

She furrowed her brows. "You really think *that's* why I'm crying?"

Phobos frowned.

"Just go away and leave me alone," she said.

"I came to tell you that the rancher is here and wants to give us the tour."

Ellie wiped her eyes and sniffed as she stood from the lower bunkbed. She didn't like the way Phobos was watching her, as if he took pleasure in her pain. She missed the man who would do anything to make her feel safe and loved, who'd tell the corniest jokes to offset the impact he had on her as the god of fear.

She recalled the first time she'd met Deacon, the satyr, and how she had grabbed Phobos's arm in fear. Phobos had made her laugh by saying that for once he wasn't the scariest thing in the room. When Deacon had sarcastically said, "You're hilarious," Phobos had turned to her and had said, "I told you."

Thinking about that moment now made her giggle as she followed Phobos from the room.

He glanced back at her. "What's so funny?"

"Something you said a couple of months ago. I miss the days when you used to make me laugh."

Phobos said nothing in reply as he joined his brothers at the door, where Mr. Garcia was waiting.

CHAPTER TWO

The Homestead

You already cleaned up the place," Mr. Garcia said at the door. He was shorter than the rest of them—about five-foot-eight—and broad. The hair that curled from beneath his straw cowboy hat was gray. His dark brows and dark eyes were handsome, reminding Phobos of Jaquelyn's. He was fit and strong, with the appearance of someone who worked hard every day of his life.

"It didn't take long," Ellie said. "Thanks for the supplies, Mr. Garcia."

"You're welcome, Ellie. And please call me Danny."

"Thanks, Danny." She followed him from the door and out onto the pea gravel. "This is a beautiful place you have."

Phobos and his brothers followed, too.

"*Muchas gracias.* It's been in my family for many generations."

"I can't wait to see it," Cupid said. "How many horses do you have?"

"Five. They're in their stables. I'll show them to you in a moment."

"My brother is a big fan of horses," Deimos said. "And he has a way with them, too."

"That's what Artemis said. I can't tell you how glad I am that she thought of bringing you here."

That makes one of us, Phobos thought.

"Most of the time, my wife and daughter and I can manage the place on our own—it's hard work, but we can do it, you know—except in the fall, when things get busy. That's when we calve, cut and bale hay, and chop wood for the winter."

Phobos wasn't familiar with the verb, "to calve," but he didn't want to expose his ignorance by asking the rancher what it meant.

"Let me show you around the homestead before we go out and see the rest of the place."

"The homestead?" Ellie asked.

As Danny walked down the dirt driveaway toward the well, he said, "That's what we call this area, where we spend most of our time. It's bordered on three sides by pasture and, to the south, by the main road."

Phobos glanced around, missing his god vision.

"It's important that you know the names of the fences," Danny said. "We have three that run east to west and seven that run north to south. You came in through the *south fence*. The fence that borders the northern acres is the *north fence*."

Phobos wished they could hear this lecture in shade. He prayed to Helios, begging him to tone it down a little.

"The fence at the back of the homestead divides the northern acres from the southern and runs right down the center of the property, cutting it in half. Guess what we call that fence."

"The *middle fence*?" Ellie asked.

"The *center fence*," Deimos guessed.

"That's right," Danny said to Deimos. "The *center fence*."

"That's what I was going to say," Phobos teased his brother.

"Sure, you were," Ellie said with a smile, but he ignored her.

Chuckling, Danny took off his hat, mopped his forehead with a rag he carried in his back pocket, and returned his hat to his head. "So, now you know the names of the three fences that run east to west."

"South, north, and center," Cupid repeated. "That's easy enough."

Phobos found this "tour" somewhat tedious. The rancher reminded him of Deimos, who spent too much time on too many details.

"We have seven fences that run north to south," Danny said. "As you might guess, the fences on the outskirts of my property are the *west fence* and the *east fence*."

"Easy enough," Cupid said again.

"We have four pastures. The homestead sits between the east and west pastures. On the other side of that barn, the northern pastures are divided into the northwest and northeast pastures. We call the fence between them the *northern divide*."

"That's cute," Ellie said.

Danny nodded. "The fence between the homestead and the west pasture is called the *west homestead fence*, and the one between the homestead and the east pasture is called the…"

"*East homestead fence*," Ellie finished.

"Exactly," Danny said. "Beyond the east pastures, we have hayfields. The fence that runs north to south between the east pastures and the hayfields is called the *hayfield fence*."

Phobos stifled a yawn and began to think he'd enjoy manual labor better than this lecture.

"Beyond the west pastures on that hill is uncleared land. It serves two purposes: it provides firewood for the winter and extra revenue during hunting season, when we lease it out. Artemis has hunted there for as long as I can remember."

Phobos was sure that Deimos was trying to predict the name of that last fence. He egged him on by saying, "Deimos, what do you suppose that fence is called?"

"You'll never guess," Danny said. "Don't even try."

"That sounds like a challenge," Phobos said, trying to incite Deimos.

"The *deer fence*?" Deimos guessed. "Or the *hunting fence*?"

"Good tries," Danny said with a laugh, "but this name won't make sense to you at first. It's called the *D.C. fence*."

"Why?" Ellie asked.

"My grandparents started calling it that back in the late 80's, when Christina and I were dating in high school. I'd take her for picnics out there and try to impress her by carving our initials into some of the trees. *Abuelo* noticed and came home one night, asking why we had so many D.C. trees. He knew why. It hadn't been hard for him to put two and two together. He enjoyed teasing me, like you kids enjoy teasing each other. Ever since then, they called it the *D.C. fence*."

"That's a sweet story," Ellie said.

Phobos resisted the urge to roll his eyes. He didn't like being referred to as a "kid." He could tell Deimos was equally put off; however, Cupid seemed pleased. Perhaps he was remembering the day that he shot the hearts of Danny and Christina.

Even though he knew his brother was sorry, Phobos still resented Cupid for putting Ellie's life before the happiness of his own brothers by shooting them. Then Cupid had made matters worse by having their powers stripped so Cupid could shoot them again with arrows of hate. Cupid had tried to make it up to them. But look where it had got them. They were literally a few feet away from a pig pen full of mud and shit.

It didn't have much in common with Mount Olympus.

Danny turned to the chicken coop. "I'm sure you noticed our chickens. We have six hens and one rooster—just enough to produce eggs and new chicks for us. As you can see, the coop is open, so the chickens can roam freely around the homestead. And Julio, over there under the tree, keeps them safe."

Danny referred to a Great Pyrenees. He had long white fur and was as large as a sheep.

"Julio's brother, Iglesias, is around here somewhere. They protect the other animals from the coyotes and snakes."

"I love their names," Ellie said. "Whose idea was it?"

"My wife, Christina. She's in love with him."

"Who?" Cupid asked.

"Julio Iglesias," Danny said. "A famous Latin singer."

Ellie went over to the tree. "Hi, Julio. You're a handsome boy."

The dog climbed to his feet and greeted her with his tongue hanging from his mouth while she stroked his long fur.

Although Phobos felt hate for the woman that had cost him and his brothers so much, the kind way she spoke to the dog reminded him of better days, and the arrow of love tingled—however briefly—in his heart.

"I think he likes you, Ellie," Cupid said.

Danny chuckled. "I'm sure he does. We have one other dog—an Australian Shepherd named Mo. He's probably inside the farmhouse. He's my wife's favorite. But just like everyone here, he has a job. He helps bring in the herd."

"What job do the pigs have?" Phobos asked, pointing to the pen beyond the coop.

"Come and meet them." Danny beckoned them to where two pigs lay in mud beneath a three-sided shelter at the back of a large twelve-by-twelve pen. "The pink one is Laverne, and the black one is Shirley."

"Hi, Laverne and Shirley," Ellie said, waving at the pigs, as if they could understand her.

"One hog will supplement my family's diet for a year. After we butcher Shirley this fall, we'll buy a second pig, so we always have two."

"Isn't it hard to eat animals that you've named and cared for?" Cupid asked.

"You get used to it," Danny said. "We give them a good life for as long as we can. Christina and my granddaughters take Laverne and Shirley for a walk every morning and let them roam around the east pasture for a while. It's the same with the chickens. We don't eat them until they stop laying, and we give them plenty of space to roam and be happy. We try to give all the animals a good life for as long as we can."

To the left of the pig pen was a corral connected to what must be the stables, for Phobos could see two horses through the openings above their stalls.

"Ready to meet the horses?" Danny asked Cupid.

"Yes, sir."

As he followed the rancher, Phobos thought it was strange to hear his brother call a *mortal* "sir."

"This first room is where we store the tack," Danny said as he led the group inside.

He showed them where the bridles, saddles, blankets, brushes, and other supplies were stored before stepping into a narrow aisle.

"We have mares in those three stalls and geldings in the stalls on each side of the tack room."

"What's a gelding?" Ellie asked.

"A castrated male," Danny said.

"Oh," she said.

Phobos laughed at the expression on her face, forgetting his hate for a moment.

Danny went to the stall opposite the tack room. "First, allow me to introduce you to our grey quarter horse, Gypsy. Come here, Gypsy. Come on, girl."

The horse crossed the stall to look at them.

"She's a beauty," Cupid said.

"My wife usually rides her. She's the oldest and gentlest, but most stubborn, of the herd—just like my wife."

Everyone laughed.

"To the right of her, we have Blondie, our Palomino. She belonged to my older daughter, Jessica, who passed away two years ago."

Phobos wasn't sure what to say to mortals when they referred to their dead loved ones, so he said nothing.

Ellie said, "I'm so sorry for your loss. I can only imagine how hard that must have been for you and your family."

"It was hard on all of us," Danny said, "but especially on Jaquelyn. She and Jessica were best friends—grew up playing together on the ranch—no other kids for miles."

"I'm so sorry," Ellie said again.

"My sweet Jessica lives on through her daughters. Rose is four, and Violet is two. Christina and I are raising them as our own."

Phobos wondered how Jessica had died, and if the father of her children was also dead.

Danny brushed a tear from his eye and went to the next stall, across from Blondie. "This is Jaquelyn's horse, Sherlock, another quarter horse. He can be fussy but is a good boy overall."

They followed Danny to the stall on the other side of Gypsy.

"This is another quarter horse, but, whereas Sherlock's coat is what you call sorrel, this color coat is called buckskin. We used to have a gelding this color that we called Buck. We call *her* Bailey."

"Hi, Bailey!" Ellie said enthusiastically. "Can I touch her, or will she not like it?"

"She'd love it," Danny said. "She'll probably turn around, so you can scratch her tailhead."

Danny's prediction was proven right. After Ellie stroked Bailey between the eyes, the horse turned in her stall to show her backside.

"I'll scratch your back if you scratch mine," Ellie teased, as she reached over to scratch the horse.

The phrase reminded Phobos of a time when he and Ellie had exchanged back rubs. It had been after a swim in Cupid's pool in the dungeon. They'd dried off, wrapped themselves in robes, and had gone up to the library, where he'd made a fire. It could get cold for mortals that high in the mountains, and who didn't love a cozy fire? They'd cuddled together on the couch, and, when he'd noticed her rubbing her neck, strained from the softball game they'd played with celebrities earlier that week, he'd offered her a massage.

His hands hadn't wanted to stop touching, kneading, and groping every part of her. He and Ellie had ended up naked on the rug before the fire, close to giving in to their passions. If it hadn't been for Deimos watching beneath the helm, Phobos wouldn't have stopped himself. Ellie certainly hadn't wanted him to stop.

He hated remembering those days. What good did those memories serve except to further enrage him over his situation? He resented Hera for suggesting that Ellie be sent to the ranch with him and his brothers. He resented all the gods, including his parents, who'd done nothing to help him.

"And last, but not least, the horse I usually ride, and our other gelding, Chestnut," Danny said, pointing to the stall across from Bailey.

"An Andalusian?" Cupid asked.

"Yep," Danny said.

"Hi, Chestnut," Ellie said.

Cupid leaned over the wall and stroked Chestnut's neck. "How long do they stay boarded each day?"

"Noon until dusk, from April to September, to keep them out of the heat," Danny said.

"They stay out all night?" Cupid asked.

"Yes—unless it's storming. Then we'll bring them in. We run the opposite schedule from October through March. We bring them in at dusk and turn them out first thing in the morning."

"Does that mean we can't expect it to cool down until October?" Phobos asked.

Danny chuckled. "That's about right. We usually get our first cold front then, but you never know in the fall in southwest Texas what the weather will be like from one day to the next. We sometimes have eighty-degree temperatures as late as Christmas day."

"I guess I won't be dreaming of a white Christmas," Ellie said playfully.

Her words surprised Phobos. She had told the other gods on Mount Olympus that they could kill her after three months, when she would revert to a mortal by not claiming her purpose. Why was she thinking about Christmas? She'd be dead by then, unless she'd changed her mind.

The arrow of hate in Phobos demanded revenge and compelled him to wish for her death; but the other arrow, though not as strong, made him desperate for her to live. Phobos was conflicted, which frustrated him and made it that much easier for the arrow of hate to dominate his heart.

CHAPTER THREE

The Ranch

Ellie hoped she would get the chance to ride a horse. Except for Pegasus, she'd only done so once, when she was little, and she could barely remember it.

"That completes your tour of the stables. Any questions?"

"Will we be riding?" Ellie asked.

"Absolutely," Danny said. "I hope you're okay with that."

"I can't wait," she said.

"Come on, let me show you the main barn."

Ellie and the brothers followed Danny from the stables to a big metal barn that was almost as wide as the homestead.

The rancher opened the tall, wide, corrugated steel doors. "This may look like one big building back here, but it isn't. We call this center building the cattle barn or the main barn. We have stalls along the perimeter for when we need to separate one of the cattle from the herd. Sometimes they get sick, or sometimes we isolate a calf, or we'll put a calf with its mother. We have two milk goats that we milk in here. Sometimes we milk a cow who's lost her calf. In mid-September, we'll fill this open space up with anywhere from fifteen to twenty yearlings. This year it's seventeen, God willing. Then we put them through the chute and load them on the trailer to sell to the feedlots."

"What's a feedlot?" Ellie asked.

"Ranches that specialize in finishing the cattle for auction," Danny said. "They don't breed and calve like we do here. They're usually bigger operations that buy yearlings from many smaller ranches like mine and then fatten the cattle with grain before auctioning them off."

"So, except in September, the barn is usually empty, like this?" Phobos asked.

"It's not empty," Danny said. "I've got one heifer with a lame leg that needs to heal and another that has an infected wound. They stay in the stalls until the vet clears them for grazing."

Ellie walked over to the stalls and said hello to the two sick cows. They seemed sad not to be out with their friends. "I'm sorry you don't feel well."

"How many cows do you have?" Cupid asked as he followed Ellie.

"We try to maintain about fifty head—give or take a few. Currently, we're at forty-nine."

"What's that building on the other side of that pen?" Deimos asked.

"That's the haybarn. We grow, cut, and bale our own hay for the winter. In fact, we'll get started next week."

"And the building on the right?" Cupid asked.

"That's the tractor barn. Come on, I'll show you."

Danny closed the big doors of the main barn. Then Ellie and the brothers followed him as he went to the building on the right and opened those doors, so they could look inside. It was a third of the size of the main barn with a tractor, an old truck, and other farming machines and implements.

"This tractor is on its last leg," Danny said. "It's over ten years old and hasn't needed much maintenance until recently. Over there are the attachments for cutting, raking, and baling the hay. Those all work fine."

"That pickup looks older than the tractor," Phobos said. "Does it still run?"

"Oh, yeah. Delores was my first truck. I got her new when I was seventeen. That was back when my grandparents ran things and the ranch was a much bigger and more profitable operation than it is today."

"What changed?" Cupid asked.

"I won't bother you with our financial struggles. Suffice it to say that life happened, and priorities changed."

Ellie's curiosity was piqued. She wondered if she could uncover what had happened. She knew what is was like to be born into poverty, but she couldn't imagine what it must feel like to start out strong and fall into hard times.

"Believe it or not, we still use Delores to feed the cows in winter. We fill up the bed with bales of hay and throw them off the back."

"And what's that corner building for?" Deimos asked. "The one across from the stables?"

"That's where we keep the dung heap," Danny said. "You can't tell it from here, but it only has three sides. It's open to the north, so the smell is directed away from the homestead. We access it through this slider here. We shovel the manure from all the pens and stalls into a wheelbarrow and deposit it in there. Then we sell it."

"Seriously?" Ellie asked, wondering who in their right mind would pay for shit.

"Yes, ma'am," Danny said. "It makes great fertilizer. About twice a month, local farmers bring their tractors right up the dirt road to these doors and buy the dung by the load."

"Nothing goes to waste," Cupid pointed out.

"Not a thing. Everybody has a job, and nothing goes to waste." Danny closed the tractor barn. "Ready to check out the land?"

When they reached the pickup, Ellie offered to sit in the back seat with two of the boys, but Phobos and Deimos insisted that she take the front bucket seat—and not to be nice.

It hurt her that they couldn't stand to be near her.

She fought tears as Danny turned the truck around and drove toward the main road. She tried to focus on the things they passed—the shack, the well, and, beyond it, the clothesline, where their bedding flapped in the gentle breeze. Then they drove between the garage and the house, where the dirt driveaway curved in front of the house and past a vegetable garden before crossing the pond.

When Ellie looked at the water more closely, she noticed it wasn't a pond, but a freshwater pool filled by the stream running downhill from the west. She also noticed two ducks bathing near the bridge.

"You have ducks, too?" she asked.

"They come and go," Danny said. "My wife takes the grandkids to feed them in the mornings. The grandkids love them."

Ellie wished she could feed the ducks, too, but she had a feeling she would be shoveling dung, instead.

"That tank is full of catfish," Danny added. "The girls love to fish. If you want to fish in your free time, you're welcome. We keep the rods and reels and tackle in the garage, where we park our vehicles, across from the house. The fish don't usually bite in the heat of the day, so you'll want to go early or late."

"What do you use for bait?" Phobos asked.

"We have a worm farm near the garden," Danny said. "Catching the worms is part of the fun for the grandkids."

"Sounds like a fun life to me," Ellie said—a lot more fun than the childhood she had.

Danny stopped in front of the gate. "Would one of you boys mind opening and closing the gate?"

Cupid hopped out of the truck. Ellie knew he blamed himself for their punishment, but she hoped Phobos and Deimos wouldn't let him work himself to death trying to make it up to them.

While they waited, Ellie glanced back at the house and noticed all the junk had been removed from the front porch. "Where did all that stuff go—the stuff that was on your front porch?"

"I donated what I could and took the rest to the dump," Danny said. "I was just getting ready to load it onto the back of my pickup when Artemis came to the door."

"We could have helped you," Ellie said.

"I wanted you to get settled in. Besides, I'll have plenty for you to do in the coming months."

Danny pulled through the open gate and waited for Cupid to close it. Then Cupid climbed into the backseat beside Deimos, and Danny turned onto the main road.

"That there to your right is the west pasture. You can sometimes catch fish from the spring. In the summers, my wife takes the kids floating on innertubes there, because the water runs fast, unless we haven't had a lot of rain. I drop Christina and the girls off where the center meets the D.C. fence, and the girls float all the way down to the west homestead fence, just in front of the house there, where it runs into the tank."

"That sounds like a blast!" Ellie said, hoping she'd get a chance to do it.

"The girls love it, though they don't get to do it as often as they'd like."

"Do you work every day?" Ellie asked.

"We have to," Danny said. "The animals need to be fed every day. But we do take off on Sunday afternoons. We go to mass after lunch and take it easy for the rest of the day. That's another reason why you found me at home today. We'd just returned from church. By the way, you're welcome to join us, if you want. Your Sunday afternoons are yours, however you want to spend them."

Danny was driving slowly on the shoulder of the main road, to allow others to pass him—though Ellie saw only one other truck go by. As Danny drove, he said, "The uncleared land is on the highest hill for miles. You can also see the northwest pasture from here."

"It's beautiful," Ellie said.

"The homestead is relatively flat, with the farmhouse built on slightly higher ground than the surrounding buildings. Everything my great grandparents did was strategically planned."

"How so?" Deimos asked from the back.

"For example, the hayfields are planted on the lowest elevation, downstream, for better irrigation. They also built the farmhouse to face the south. Most of the winds come from the south, especially in summer, making it pleasant to sit out on the front porch in the evenings. The south winds also blow the animal smells away from the house."

"That was smart," Phobos said.

"They chose the west pasture for fall and winter grazing because it's a valley, see? The high elevation of the northwest pasture protects the cattle from the northern winds that come during winter."

"That's interesting," Deimos said.

"The cattle graze the northwest pasture in the summers, because it's cooler on the hilltop, and because that pasture has the most trees and running water."

"I can see them," Ellie said of the cows. "Why do they bunch together like that, when there's so much room?"

"Believe it or not, there's usually an alpha cow that the others want to stay close to."

"Are they all cows?" Phobos asked.

"Cows and their calves. The males are castrated not long after birth. We keep our bull, Rusty, separated from the herd until breeding season."

"When's that?" Cupid asked.

"Late winter, early spring." Danny pointed to Ellie's window. "That's the land we lease to hunters. We have a few deer blinds and feeders, but you can't see them from the road."

"How many acres do you have?" Phobos asked.

"A little over two hundred."

"You can see for miles from up here," Ellie said. "It's beautiful country."

"I feel very fortunate. I pray to God I never lose it."

Danny turned right on another road that ran along the western side of his property. Since there was nothing to see here but trees, he drove on the main part of the road at the regular speed.

Ellie wished she could say she was glad to be there, but under the circumstances, she'd rather be back at Cupid's castle or playing for the Seminoles.

"What did you folks do before you…ran into trouble with the law?"

Ellie glanced back at the three brothers, curious to hear their answers.

Cupid said, "I took care of the family horses and helped my mother with, uh, with a matchmaking service."

"So, that's why they call you Cupid."

"Exactly," Cupid said.

"And what about you, Phobos and Deimos? Did you help around the family stables, too?"

Ellie smiled, enjoying the view of the twin gods squirming in their seats as they tried to explain what they did.

"We worked for the family," Deimos said. "But in a different capacity."

"Yeah," Phobos said. "We did a lot of odd and end jobs, providing support for the others."

"Sounds like you're jacks of all trades—exactly what a ranch hand needs to be."

Ellie turned back to the windshield, impressed that they'd managed to pull it off.

"What about you, Ellie?" Danny asked.

"I just finished my second year of college at Florida state, where I pitched for the Seminoles."

"That's right! Jaquelyn told me about that. She said you won the world series for your team." Danny turned right onto another main road.

Ellie blushed. "It was a team effort."

"How did you go from being a superstar to a parolee—if you don't mind my asking?"

Ellie felt her face get hot. She *did* mind him asking. How could she possibly explain that she'd been taken by gods, turned into one, and then stripped of her powers? "Suffice it to say that life happened, and priorities shifted," she finally said.

"*Touché*," Danny said with a laugh. "I guess I had no business asking. I'm just curious to know more about the people I'll be living and working with for the next six months. By the way, there's a good view of the herd."

The cattle hung out together beneath a cluster of trees near the spring, not far from the north fence.

"Artemis wasn't completely honest with you when she called us parolees," Phobos said.

Ellie gasped and glanced back, her stomach turning into a knot.

Cupid gave Phobos a look of warning.

Danny frowned. "Then why would she say you were?"

"Because she's our aunt, and we disappointed her," Phobos said. "We let our whole family down. They wanted to teach us a lesson."

"It was my fault," Cupid said. "The others were innocent, but we all got blamed for my bad decisions."

"I wonder why Artemis felt the need to lie," Danny said.

"She probably thought you'd be easier on us if you knew the truth," Deimos said.

"Or maybe she didn't want you to know about our family drama," Phobos said.

"But the truth is," Cupid said, "I'm the only one who should have been sent here. I think the others were sent to further punish me."

"You sound like someone who carries around a lot of guilt and remorse," Danny said.

Ellie glanced at Cupid and noticed tears welling in his eyes.

"Yes, sir," Cupid said.

"He was trying to save my life," Ellie blurted out. "He had good intentions, and his parents hadn't been totally honest with him."

"It's complicated," Deimos added.

"Well, thank you for sharing that with me," Danny said. "We don't ever have to talk about it again. By the way, that's the northeast pasture. Rusty is out there somewhere, but I don't see him."

Ellie looked for the bull. She didn't see him either. She wondered if he was lonely, out there all by himself.

"And now we're coming up to the hayfield. This will need to be cut in a few weeks. Have any of you ever cut and baled hay?"

"No, but we're fast learners," Deimos said.

They were quiet for the rest of the drive. Ellie wondered if Danny was trying to decide whether he believed their story, and if he had second thoughts about accepting their help.

When Danny stopped outside the southern fence, Ellie offered to open and close the gate this time. It was easy to push open. While she stood there, waiting for Danny to drive through, she took a deep breath and sighed. The wind had picked up, and the sun had moved behind clouds, making it feel cooler and more pleasant than it had been earlier.

Danny waited for her to climb back in. When they passed the tank, Ellie noticed an older woman with two little girls in the garden. They waved to the pickup as Danny drove by. Ellie waved back.

"That's my wife and granddaughters. They're picking vegetables for our supper," Danny said.

Ellie imagined it must feel satisfying to produce your own food and to live off the land. She was nervous about doing something unfamiliar to her, but she was also excited. And her determination to win back the hearts of Phobos and Deimos had only grown stronger.

CHAPTER FOUR

The Streams

After Danny dropped them off at the shack, Ellie walked over to the clothesline and touched the bedding.

"It's dry," she said. "That didn't take long."

"Thank Helios," Cupid said, joining her as she collected the sheets and blankets.

Phobos wasn't happy to see her handling his bedding.

"I thought I told you I didn't want you anywhere near my bedding," he said.

"I'm just trying to help. Jeez Louise."

"Go ahead then," Phobos said. "I'm going for a swim. Anybody else game?"

Phobos was careful not to make eye contact with Ellie. He made it clear that she wasn't invited.

Cupid seemed irritated at him. "You go ahead."

"I'll go," Deimos said.

They grabbed towels from the shack and went through the gate to the west pasture, where Danny had said that his wife and grandkids liked to ride innertubes down the stream. They found a shady spot and stripped down.

Deimos stuck a toe into the water. "It's colder than it looks."

"Good."

Phobos couldn't recall ever feeling as hot and sweaty as he had today.

He jumped in, feet first, and went all the way under.

When he popped back up, he was several feet downstream of where he'd jumped in. "It's deep in the middle, and the current's strong."

"I see that." Deimos sat on a long flat rock only a few inches beneath the surface. "Enjoy your trip."

Phobos soon realized there was no point trying to fight the current, so he allowed himself to be carried downstream. He floated on his back, with his face in the direction he was going, and enjoyed the views of the clear blue sky and rolling hills. After five or ten minutes, the water became shallow again. He glanced back at Deimos and was surprised to find at least a hundred meters between them.

Feeling refreshed, Phobos climbed from the stream and headed back, uphill, on foot, toward Deimos, who was already stepping back into his clothes. When Deimos picked up Phobos's clothes and towel, Phobos thought Deimos meant to meet him halfway. Instead, Deimos headed back to the gate.

"That turd," Phobos muttered.

Phobos really didn't care who saw him naked. You don't grow up among gods with x-ray vision feeling modest about your body.

When he walked into the shack, still naked and dripping, the look on Ellie's face was deeply satisfying to him. If he'd thought she'd given up on love, the look on her face told him otherwise.

Let her burn, he thought.

Phobos grabbed his towel from his laughing brother and dried his junk in front of her, enjoying every bit of the blush in her cheeks as she averted her eyes, only to glance his way again.

Then he grabbed his clothes from Deimos and carried them to his room.

As he passed Ellie, he glared at her. "What are you looking at?"

"Come on, Ellie," Cupid said. "It's our turn to go for a swim."

After they'd gone, Deimos said, "You show no mercy, do you, brother?"

"Why should I?"

"What's the point?"

"It feels good. *That's* the point."

When Phobos reached his room and saw that Ellie and Cupid had made his bed, he felt a tiny bit guilty for the way he'd treated her. Then he blamed her for making him feel guilty.

"Self-righteous bitch," he muttered as he lay down to rest before dinner.

Ellie followed Cupid from the shack.

"Let's go to the northeast pasture," Ellie suggested. "Maybe the current won't be as strong up there."

"But isn't that where Rusty is grazing?"

"So? Jaquelyn said he wouldn't bother us. And besides, he couldn't hurt me any more than your brothers have."

"Keep reminding yourself that it's Eris's *arrow* making them behave so cruelly toward you," Cupid said as he opened the gate.

"But then I'm reminded that it was *your* arrow that made them behave as though they loved me."

"The arrow of love only works if there's a natural inclination."

"Is that true of the arrow of hate?"

When he didn't answer, she glanced back at him as they walked up the hill toward a cluster of trees. "It is, isn't it?"

"Yes, but love and hate are two sides of passion. They resent you for not choosing between them, even though it's my fault."

"Quit saying that. I'm tired of hearing it."

"But it's true."

"Let's just make the best of this, okay? It's beautiful here, isn't it? I mean, look at it." She pointed to the stream beneath the trees. "We get to ride horses and be with nature. I've never lived like this. For me, poverty meant Ramen noodles, Spam, hot dogs, and other cheap, processed foods—not fresh eggs and vegetables. It meant loud neighbors in cheap government housing with thin walls, not acres and acres of beautiful country."

"I'd like it better if it weren't so hot."

She dipped her foot in the stream. "Oooh. It feels good."

Cupid stripped down and jumped in, going all the way under.

She laughed, trying not to admire his beautiful body—he was married, after all.

When he resurfaced, she said, "How about a warning next time?"

"Fine."

"Turn around," she said.

Cupid swam upstream, away from her. She quickly stepped out of her boots and jeans and stripped down to her birthday suit, not wanting to get her underclothes wet. Then she slipped into the stream, finding a shallow spot where she could squat down until the water covered her from the neck down.

"Damn, this feels good!" she cried. "Oh, thank the gods for cold water in Texas."

The water flowed gently and sparkled beneath the late afternoon sun. The stream was clear enough for Ellie to see the shallow rocks beneath her. She swam the breaststroke, downstream, and took in the lovely views of the blue sky and rolling hills. She could even see the hay dancing in the breeze at the bottom of the hill.

"I just scraped my hand on a rock," Cupid said from a few meters away. "It's bleeding."

"You okay?"

"Yeah. It didn't hurt that much, but I'm used to healing right away. This sucks."

"Sorry, but you better get used to it."

"Yeah, and I better be more careful with my body while I don't have powers."

"You still can't die, right?"

"All gods can die."

"I meant forever. You'd still come back to your body."

"Once my body healed itself."

"Would it, without your powers?"

"Yes, because I'm still immortal—that part hasn't changed. It's the same for you, now, too."

"Maybe we could find a way to hang out in Tartarus until this punishment is over."

"They'd never let us get away with it."

Ellie laughed. "Death would be too easy."

"There are certainly worse things than death—that's for sure."

Ellie dipped her head back in the water to wet her hair. "Oh, this feels so nice. I could stay here all evening."

"I'm starving. That's another thing I'll have to get used to."

"I'm sleepy. Maybe I should take a nap before dinner."

"That's not a bad idea. Should we go?"

"You first."

Ellie turned around to give Cupid privacy while he dressed.

"Ready."

"Okay. You turn around."

Ellie kept her eyes on the back of Cupid's head as she quickly dried herself off and stepped back into her clothes.

"Done," she said, as she slipped on her boots.

"Hey, it's Rusty," Cupid said, pointing to the bull standing about twenty meters away.

"Hi, Rusty!" Ellie said, waving. "You're friendly, aren't you?"

The bull snorted.

"That doesn't sound good," Cupid whispered.

The bull swiped his front hoof through the terrain three times, as if he were about to charge.

"Run!" Cupid said, taking off.

Ellie ran, glancing back to see Rusty gaining on them. She laughed and shrieked out loud, feeling delirious, like when she rode a rollercoaster. "He's right behind us. Should we split up?"

"No," he said. "Our chances are better if we stay together."

Whether it was because his powers had been diminished, or because she'd been made into an immortal, she didn't know, but she reached the gate first and unlatched it as quickly as she could. The bull stopped about five feet away as Cupid ran through, and Ellie slammed the gate closed.

"That was close!" she said, panting but feeling exuberant.

"Maybe we'll avoid that pasture in the future," Cupid said with a grin. He was bent over, trying to catch his breath.

Rusty was staring at Ellie.

"What's your deal, Rusty?" she said.

He turned around and walked away.

"Story of my life," she said with a laugh. "Even the bull hates me."

"Not everyone hates you," Cupid said. "Come on. Let's go lie down for a bit."

They returned to the shack to find Phobos and Deimos asleep on their bunks. Ellie was glad for the break from Deimos's avoidance and Phobos's cruelty. She lay down on the bottom bunk as Cupid climbed to the top. She enjoyed the fresh scent of the clean bedding and of the evening breeze blowing through the windows. Still determined to make the best of her situation, to find a way back into the twins' hearts, she closed her eyes and smiled.

She felt as though she had just dozed off when a knock on the door awakened her.

"Hello?"

It was Jaquelyn's voice.

Cupid jumped from the top bunk. She followed him to the main room.

"We're about to turn out the horses," Jaquelyn said. "My parents thought you might want to watch."

"Thanks," Cupid said as he followed Jaquelyn.

Ellie went, too. She glanced back at the sight of the twins, looking sleepy, disheveled, and sexy as hell, coming behind her.

It was already dusk as she followed Jaquelyn to the stables, where Danny was opening the stall doors.

The horses knew exactly where to go. All but Gypsy were in a hurry. The gray quarter horse took her time, giving Cupid and Ellie a chance to stroke her.

They followed the horses from the stables and watched them go out to pasture. Sherlock, Blondie, and Bailey trotted toward the distance, looking pleased to be free. To Ellie, they were majestic and a symbol of everything she longed to be.

Chestnut and Gypsy stood near the fence munching on grass and staring at the humans.

"They're curious about you," Danny said.

"We're curious about them," Phobos said with a laugh.

Deimos scratched his chin. "Did you know that horses were first introduced to humans in the year…"

"Not now, Professor Deimos," Phobos teased.

Ellie smiled, happy to see the boys acting more like themselves.

"Horses have been here as long as people have," Danny said.

Deimos lifted his finger. "Actually…"

"Didn't Adam and Eve come first?" Jaquelyn asked her father.

"Yes, *mija*. My mistake."

"Her name was Pandora," Deimos said.

"That's Greek for *Eve*," Cupid said, which Ellie knew wasn't true.

"Well," Danny said. "That's enough talk about the beginning of time. Let's eat."

CHAPTER FIVE

The Farmhouse

The farmhouse hadn't looked like much on the outside, but on the inside, Phobos was impressed by the amount of space there was and how efficiently the family used it.

They'd followed Danny and Jaquelyn from the east homestead fence, where they'd admired the horses as they were turned out to pasture, and in through the back of the house, where a wooden porch led to a set of old French doors. The porch looked like a great place to hang out and watch the sunset in the evenings. It had a hammock on one side and a porch swing on the other.

Inside, they walked directly into a dining area—nothing fancy, but comfortable enough, with wooden floors and a wooden beam running the length of the high ceiling. There were two antique farm tables on each side of the rectangular room, and each sat about ten people.

At one of the tables, two little girls sat side by side on a bench before plates of chopped up food. One of them was humming while the other seemed to be playing a game with her vegetables.

"Come in, come in!" an older woman, whom Phobos presumed was Christina, said as they entered. She was tiny, no more than five-foot-two, with short black and gray hair and dark eyes. She wiped her hands on her apron as she stepped from the kitchen. "Please have a seat wherever you'd like. You can sit with us, or you can have the other table to yourselves. It's totally up to you. Just make yourselves comfortable, and I'll bring you a plate."

Ellie sat on the bench across from the little girls, so Phobos sat at the other table. Deimos followed him, and, as Phobos might have predicted, Cupid sat beside Ellie.

While he waited for his plate, Phobos glanced around the open floor plan. The interior was laid out well but needed repairs and updating. The paint was dull, the wallpaper outdated, and the furniture torn and stained.

Straight ahead from where he sat was a grouping of chairs and sofas around a brick fireplace. Opposite it and adjacent to the other table was the kitchen, where Jaquelyn and Christina were busy making plates on the other side of the kitchen counter. Danny stood at the counter pouring something from a pitcher into glasses of ice.

Beyond the kitchen and living area, the front door was flanked by walls of windows. Phobos imagined the bedrooms and baths must be accessed by the doorways on either side of them.

Christina took plates to Cupid and Ellie while Jaquelyn served Phobos and Deimos.

Phobos smiled up at the pretty girl. "Thank you."

Her face was soon covered by the most spectacular blush.

"You're welcome," she said before returning to the kitchen.

Danny delivered glasses of iced tea to everyone, and then the three servers made their own plates and sat at the other table with Cupid and Ellie. Christina sat on the bench between her grandkids, while Danny took the chair at the head of the table at the far end. Jaqueline sat in the chair at the opposite end to Danny with her back to Phobos and Deimos.

Phobos wondered if she sat there because that was her usual place, of if she wanted to be as close to him as possible while eating at the family table.

"Let's pray," Danny said.

Everyone at the other table held hands, but when Deimos reached across the table for Phobos's, he smirked and pulled away. Although the mortals thanked someone called *Father* for their food, Phobos believed that Demeter and Hestia were the ones responsible, so he thanked *them*, instead, and began to eat.

"You've already met my daughter, Jaquelyn," Danny said. "This is my wife, Christina, and my granddaughters, Rose and Violet."

"Hello," Rose said.

The littler girl, Violet, didn't look up from her plate and her game with her vegetables.

"Christina, this is Ellie—the one Jaquelyn was telling us about—and Cupid. They call him that because he worked for his mother's match-making service."

"How cute," Christina said. "It's nice to meet you."

"It's my pleasure," Cupid said.

"And those boys are Phobos and Deimos. I still don't know which is which."

Deimos raised his hand. "I'm Deimos."

"It's nice to meet all of you," Christina said. "You couldn't have come at a better time. Things will get very busy for us in the coming months."

Phobos wanted to say that he'd rather be in Tartarus than working on a hot Texas ranch full of animal shit and bugs, but he smiled and gave the woman a nod of appreciation.

As he took his first bite of the pork ribs, a dog with white and black fur approached and stared at him.

"No, Moseby-Mo!" Christina scolded. "You know better than that. Go lay down."

The dog hung his head at Phobos for another moment and then left the dining room.

"I thought his name was Mo," Ellie said.

Jaquelyn grinned. "It is. That's just my mom's name for him."

"He's a cute boy," Ellie said.

"Do you have any pets at home?" Christina asked Ellie.

"No, ma'am. I love animals, though. I had two cats for a while, but I couldn't keep them. I really miss them a lot. They were so sweet." Ellie gave Phobos and Deimos a pathetic glance.

Phobos resented the reminder of those lazy, joyful days when he cuddled with Ellie in bed as she stroked and doted on him.

Ellie chuckled. "One time, I let them take a *bath* with me. They were so cute, covered in suds. They really were sweet."

"Mimi, can I take a bath with Mo?" Rose asked.

"No, Rosie-Ro," Christina said.

"Please?" the little girl begged.

"Maybe some other day. Now eat your supper, like a good girl."

Rose smiled at Ellie from across the table, and Ellie winked at her.

Phobos was irritated by how cute Ellie was when she was playful. He tried to avoid looking in her direction for the rest of the meal.

Ellie couldn't believe how tasty the food was. The pork was tender and perfectly seasoned. The corn on the cobb was sweet and buttery. The scalloped potatoes were creamy. And even the little green things she didn't recognize were delicious.

"What are these green things?" she asked.

"Brussels sprouts," Christina said. "Do you like them?"

Ellie's mouth dropped open. "These are *brussels sprouts*? No way!"

Jaquelyn and Danny laughed. Even the little girls giggled.

Christina smiled wide. "Why don't you believe me?"

"My mama made them once, and they were *terrible*. I think she boiled them too long. They were so mushy and gross. Ever since then, I've always thought I hated brussels sprouts. But these are so good!"

"I don't like them boiled either," Danny said.

"These are super easy to make," Christina said. "I just cut them in quarters, toss them in salt and pepper and olive oil, and then broil them for about six or seven minutes."

Ellie took another bite. "This is my new favorite vegetable—though everything tastes good. Thank you so much."

Except for the two months she lived with Cupid, she hadn't eaten food that was truly delicious. At Florida state, she lived on cafeteria mac and cheese, chicken nuggets, and hamburgers.

"What else did your mother cook at home?" Christina asked.

"She wasn't much of a cook," Ellie said. "My grandma was, but my mom never learned, I guess. Grandma would make the most delicious gumbo, red beans and rice, fried catfish, and shrimp and grits. I miss her cooking. She died when I was seven. From then on, it was canned vegetables, hot dogs, canned soups, Spaghetti-o's, frozen pizzas, and Spam. I'm not exaggerating."

"What's Spam?" Cupid asked.

"Canned meat," Ellie said. "At least, I *think* it was meat."

Everyone at her table laughed, even the two little girls. Ellie glanced at Phobos and Deimos, but they ignored her.

"Mimi?" Rose asked. "Are you going to die?"

"One day, *mija*," Christina said. "But not for a long time."

"My grandma was really sick," Ellie said. "But your mimi is perfectly healthy."

"My *mama* died," Rose said.

Ellie wished she hadn't mentioned her grandma's death. "I'm so sorry."

"That's okay," Rose said. "My Mimi's my mama now. Right, Mimi?"

"That's right, *mija*." Christina kissed the top of Rose's head. "Now, eat your supper."

The mention of Rose's mother's death had soured the mood. Ellie felt horrible.

"This ranch is so beautiful," Ellie said. "Cupid and I went swimming in the northeast pasture, and the water felt amazing!"

Cupid laughed. "But Rusty wasn't too happy to see us."

Ellie laughed, too. "He chased us out."

"I'm sorry about that," Danny said. "I should have warned you not to run. He wouldn't have chased you if you'd waited for him to walk off."

Ellie wasn't so sure about that, but she said nothing.

"How was the swimming in the west pasture?" Jaquelyn asked Deimos.

Phobos lifted his brows. "How did you know we went swimming there?"

"I saw you. The flow is pretty fast right now, isn't it?"

Deimos smiled, making Ellie wish it had been for her. "Phobos had a nice trip, didn't you, bro'?"

"It *was* nice," he said, giving Jaquelyn a flirtatious grin. "Have you gone swimming there lately?"

"No, but I should."

"Join us next time," Phobos said.

Phobos's flirting was making Ellie sick. She put down her fork, unable to finish her plate.

"Save room for dessert," Christina said. "I made fresh blueberry pie. The girls helped me pick the blueberries this afternoon, didn't you girls?"

The little girls nodded.

Rose patted her belly. "I *ate* some, too."

"Were they good?" Ellie asked.

Rose nodded. "Are you going to eat some?"

"I'm too full," Ellie said. "But thank you. I think I need to lie down."

"Before you go," Danny said, "I wanted to give y'all the lowdown on tomorrow's jobs."

"Sure," Ellie said.

"We eat breakfast at six o'clock, just before sunrise," Danny said. "I'll have Jaquelyn ring the dinner bell on the back porch when she and the girls have collected the eggs."

Ellie wasn't sure she could eat that early. *Before sunrise? Jeez Louise.*

"Next, we clean all the stalls and pens," Danny said. "We shovel dung and take it to the heap."

"Even the pig pen?" Phobos asked.

"Yes, sir," Danny said. "Christina and the girls walk the pigs after breakfast, and that's where we start."

Ellie tried not to laugh at the expression on Phobos's face.

"After we get the stalls clean and fresh hay spread, we bring in the horses for grooming. Mo brings them in. And the horses know that they'll get oats. We give them special feed after we groom them, to be sure they're getting enough vitamins and minerals."

Ellie couldn't wait to groom the horses.

"After we feed and water the horses, the pigs, and the goats, it's our turn to eat," Danny said.

"What about the dogs?" Ellie asked. "When do they eat?"

"I feed them before breakfast," Jaquelyn said, "when I feed the chickens and gather the eggs. The dogs eat again before bedtime."

Ellie raised her brows. "What time do you wake up?"

"Five thirty. That's why I'm ready to hit the sack after supper. You will be too, tomorrow."

Christina laughed. "Just wait. You'll probably be sore, too."

"After lunch, our jobs vary," Danny continued. "This week, we'll focus on repairing the fences."

Ellie sucked in her lips. That meant they'd be standing in the afternoon heat all day.

"At dusk, we return to the homestead to turn out the horses. Then we wash up for supper. We eat at eight, which is right around sundown, as you can see, and then we clean up the dishes and go to bed."

Ellie wondered if they ever did anything else but work all day.

"We work long days," Danny said, "but we love what we do, don't we, girls? Rosie? Violet? You like taking care of the ranch?"

The two little girls nodded.

"There's nothing more satisfying," Christina said.

Jaquelyn laughed out loud. "I wouldn't go that far. I can think of a few things I'd rather do."

Everyone laughed again.

"Anyone want some pie?" Christina asked.

As Jaquelyn helped her mother serve pie to the others, Ellie asked if she could be excused.

"You want to use the bathroom first?" Danny asked. "I'll show you where it is."

Ellie was glad for the reminder. She followed the rancher across the living area to a hallway near the front of the house.

"First door on the right," Danny said.

"Thanks."

Even though the décor was outdated, like something from the late eighties or early nineties, Ellie loved the farmhouse. It wasn't Cupid's castle, but it was bigger and nicer than anyplace she'd ever lived. If Artemis thought this family was poor, Ellie thought the goddess could use an education in poverty. These people lived like kings compared to the life Ellie knew growing up—though they worked much harder than kings.

After Ellie did her business, she stared at her reflection in the mirror over the sink. How had her life changed so dramatically in two months? Jaquelyn had been surprised to hear that Ellie was no longer playing for the Seminoles. And even though Ellie missed it, her love for Phobos and Deimos made her glad for the change. Would she ever play softball again? She didn't know. For now, she only cared about winning back the hearts of the men she loved.

She had a hard time falling asleep. Still awake when the boys returned, she overheard Phobos saying what a beautiful girl Jaquelyn was.

"Be smart," Deimos said. "If you screw things up with the rancher, we might get sent someplace worse."

"I'll wait," Phobos said. "But mark my words: I'll have her before we leave."

Ellie fumed and hit her pillow, doubting she'd get any sleep at all.

CHAPTER SIX

The Dung Heap

Phobos had a difficult time falling asleep. He tossed and turned for hours, wishing he hadn't napped. He was also bothered by the fact that Ellie was sleeping a few short feet away from him in the bunk across the hall. The rooms had no doors, and he could see the bottom half of her, lying on top of the covers, in nothing but her shirt and panties.

Even though he felt an overwhelming hate for her, he hadn't forgotten the days and nights they'd spent together in Cupid's castle. He relived those memories over and over in his mind, but when he came back to the reality of the present, he felt nothing but resentment toward her again.

A logical part of him knew his hate was caused by Eris's arrow and nothing Ellie had done to deserve it. But another part of him resented the fact that she'd been unable to choose him over Deimos. Phobos had loved Ellie more than he'd ever loved another living being. He'd been hurt that she hadn't felt the same way.

For the hundredth time since he'd arrived, he prayed to Zeus and to his parents to bring him home and to restore his powers. He'd do anything.

But he knew his prayers were futile.

He lay there, listening to the crickets and the nighttime wind through the open windows. He was glad the nights were cool. The breeze circulated throughout the shack and brought relief from the day's heat.

From the window beside his bed, he could see the stars illuminating the sky. He looked for all the constellations visible on this side of the world, to distract himself from looking across the hall at Ellie.

But he still couldn't sleep. He gave in and stared at Ellie while he slipped his hand into his underwear and pleasured himself.

The whole bunkbed creaked when he moved. He tried to be quiet and discreet, but after a few short minutes, Deimos groaned, "Do that someplace else."

Too far in to quit, Phobos got up and went outside. He stood at Ellie's window, where he could see her perfectly in the moonlight. The hate he felt for her hadn't made her less beautiful to him. If anything, her beauty made him resent her even more.

He stood barefoot on the pea gravel in nothing but his briefs and moved his hand beneath the waistband. He remembered the time he had touched Ellie's breasts in the swimming pool. It didn't take long for him to finish. Then he returned to bed and, finally, to sleep.

He felt as though he had just dozed off when the dinner bell rang. He ignored it at first, but when he heard the others dressing and putting on their boots, he reluctantly climbed out of bed and did the same.

It was dark outside as they trudged across the gravel to the farmhouse. The coffee helped. But the eggs and sausage filled his hungry belly and made him long to go back to bed.

Christina put the dirty dishes into the sink to soak as the rest of them headed to the pig pen. Even the two little girls were up and ready to work.

Violet was standing on the dirt road between the well and the chicken coop by herself. Her sister was with Jaquelyn in the pig pen. Phobos noticed Violet squirming and marching until soon, she began to cry. Then he realized she was standing in a bed of ants, and they were crawling all over her.

He rushed to her, picked her up, and quickly batted the ants away while she screamed in terror.

"What are you doing?" Deimos asked.

The others soon gathered round.

"Fire ants," Phobos said. "She was standing in them."

"Come here, Vi," Christina said, as she dashed from the house. She took the little girl from Phobos. "Thank you so much… Phobos? Or Deimos?"

"Phobos."

"Thank you, Phobos."

Christina hurried into the house with the crying little girl on her hip.

"Thanks, Phobos," Danny said. "That could have been a lot worse if you hadn't stepped in to help. I need to remember to pour some hot oil on that ant bed."

"I hope she didn't get bit too many times." Phobos knocked his hands together, to make sure he was rid of the ants. He'd gotten stung in two places—his palm and thumb.

When he looked up, he noticed Ellie smiling at him. He said nothing as he followed Danny to the pig pen.

Danny put a wheelbarrow in the middle of the pen while Jaquelyn and Rose took the pigs for a walk where the horses were grazing. Once the gate was closed behind them, the others were given shovels and gloves and got to work piling the shit onto the wheelbarrow.

Phobos couldn't imagine waking up to this every morning.

They worked in silence until the pen was cleared. Then Danny handed his shovel to Cupid and said, "Follow me," as he pushed the wheelbarrow from the pen.

Phobos saw Helios coming over from the east while Danny opened the doors to the dung heap. The heap was full of flies and maggots and stunk to high heaven. Ellie covered her mouth and nose with the crook of her arm and looked as though she would vomit.

Danny put the wheelbarrow at the edge of the heap and took his shovel from Cupid. "Use your shovels to scrape the dung from the wheelbarrow."

With the five of them working, they finished in less than a minute.

Then Danny pushed the wheelbarrow to the stables, where they started again.

He'd been shoveling for only a few minutes when Phobos heard Ellie shriek. He looked over at the stall across from him to see she'd fallen in a pile of shit.

The look on her face made him bust out laughing. She surprised him by laughing, too. He was even more surprised by how good it felt to share the laugh with her.

But it didn't take long for the feelings of hate and resentment to return. He quickly got back to work.

Cupid took her hand and helped her up.

"This is so gross," she said.

"Get used to it," Danny said with a laugh. "We'll all be covered in dung before lunchtime."

"But these are my only pair of jeans," Ellie said.

"That ain't good," Danny said. "I'm sure Jaquelyn has an extra pair you can wear. Meanwhile, there's a hose you can use to spray off the dung after we finish."

Once they'd scraped the last bit of dung from the stalls, they returned to the heap and added it to the pile.

"The hardest part's behind us," Danny said. "Now we go to the main barn. I'll move the sick heifers to a fresh stall, and then we can get started."

They followed Danny and watched as he helped the heifer with the bad leg move.

"Poor thing," Ellie said. "How much longer before she heals?"

"About two more weeks," Danny said. "Not long."

Once they'd finished shoveling dung, they raked up the remaining hay, put it into the wheelbarrow, and added it to the compost bin that was between the pig pen and the garage.

Next, Danny showed them how and where to spray off the wheelbarrow, shovels, and rakes and where to store them to dry. Then he talked them through spraying off the concrete aisle in the stables and main part of the barn before handing the hose to Ellie, so she could wash off the back of her jeans.

The wet jeans hugged her bottom. When Ellie noticed Phobos staring, he quickly looked away.

Once Ellie had finished washing the dung from her jeans, Danny took the hose and showed them where to wash out and refill the water buckets for each of the horses, the goats, and the pigs. Then he suggested they all take a drink from the hose, so as not to get dehydrated.

Ellie was shocked when Deimos handed her the hose and offered her a drink first. As she took it from him, she wished she knew what was going on in his mind. Did he still have any feelings of love for her? He hadn't been as cruel to her as Phobos, but he hadn't been particularly friendly, either, until just now, when he'd offered her the hose.

After everyone had their fill of water, Danny turned off the spigot and recoiled the hose.

"Now we spread new bedding in the stalls and pens," Danny said, as he led them to the hay barn.

It took nearly an hour for them to carry the square bales of hay from the barn and spread it out in each of the stalls and pens. They started with the pig pen, so Jaquelyn and Rose could return Laverne and Shirley to their clean beds.

Then Jaquelyn and Rose helped spread hay. Rose talked the entire time.

"Will you teach me to play softball?" she asked Ellie at one point. "Jaquelyn won't, and I want to learn."

"I'd love to," Ellie said. "Do you have a softball, glove, and bat?"

"Jaquelyn does, but she won't let me play with them."

"I will if Ellie's with you," Jaquelyn said.

"Goodie!" Rose clapped her hands and smiled wide. "When, Ellie?"

"Maybe next Sunday, after church?"

"Goodie!" Rose ran to her grandpa. "Papa, Ellie's going to teach me how to play softball!"

"Just make sure she gets her work done first, girlie."

"I will," Rose said.

Once the beds were laid, Mo was called from the house to bring in the horses. Ellie perked up as she watched the Australian Shepherd run out to the east pasture and round up the herd.

All but Gypsy trotted with Mo back to the stables. The gray mare took her sweet time.

"We're running earlier than usual, thanks to y'all," Danny said to them as he brought the horses in. "Jaquelyn, why don't you and Rose go help Mimi with lunch while I show the new hands how we groom our horses?"

But I want to stay with you, Papa," Rose complained. "And Ellie."

"Do as your Papa says," Danny told her.

Before Jaquelyn took Rose's hand and left the stables, she exchanged a smile with Phobos. Ellie bit her lip and glared at him. He made her angrier by laughing.

"He's only taunting you," Cupid whispered in her ear. "Don't let him get to you."

Danny told them to grab a brush and assigned them each a horse, asking them to brush in the aisle, to keep the stalls clean.

"We'll sweep up after," he said.

Cupid got to work brushing Bailey. Ellie and the twins waited for Danny to tell them what to do. Ellie was assigned Sherlock. She started at the top, with his face and mane, and worked her way down, being sure to brush off the grass and sticker burrs. Then she checked each hoof, as she'd been told, for rocks. Sherlock didn't have any.

She enjoyed being close to the animal and found herself softly talking to him as she brushed him. She said things like, "Does that feel good?" and "You like that, don't you, Sherlock?"

"You always want to check their eyes and ears, and make sure they don't have any signs of infections," Danny said as they were finishing up. "If their eyes are red, or if you see anything oozing, let me know."

"Sherlock looks healthy," Ellie said. "Will we get to ride soon?"

"Tomorrow afternoon," Danny said. "We exercise them twice a week—on Tuesdays and Fridays, just before dusk."

Ellie clapped her hands together, feeling like Rose must have felt when she'd been told she would learn how to play softball.

Sherlock stepped away from her and snorted, looking uncomfortable.

"I'm sorry," Ellie said, realizing her clapping had frightened him.

"That's my fault," Danny said. "I should have warned you that the horses don't like sudden, loud noises they aren't used to." He rubbed Sherlock's back. "Come on, boy. In your stall."

The boys opened the stall doors for their horses, too. Ellie helped Chestnut, since Danny was soothing Sherlock. The animals drank fresh water and seemed eager for their grain.

Danny showed them how to fill their food buckets with feed, and then Cupid and Danny swept the horsehair, grass, and burrs from the aisle and into the east pasture while Ellie and the twins put away all the work gloves.

"That wasn't so bad," she said to the twins as they were leaving the barn, where they'd put the work gloves.

"Wasn't so good, either," Phobos said.

"You've got to admit, this place—the land, the horses—it's all so beautiful," she said.

"I prefer Mount Olympus," Phobos said.

"What about you, Deimos?" Ellie asked. "Do you like it here?"

"Some of it. Not all of it."

As they met Danny and Cupid near the chicken coop, Ellie wondered if Deimos included her among the things he didn't like.

"You guys did great this morning," Danny said. "We have a full hour before lunchtime. Feel free to relax until then."

Ellie filled her canteen at the well and gulped down water.

"I'm going for a swim," Cupid called out to her. "But I don't trust Rusty. I'm going to the west pasture. Want to come?"

"Yes!"

Eager to be rid of the smell of shit, she grabbed her towel from the clothesline and followed Cupid to the stream.

"Of all the places the gods could have sent us," Cupid said, "I'm glad we're here. The Garcias are a nice family, and the land and the animals are beautiful."

"I was just saying the same thing to Phobos and Deimos."

"What did they say?"

"Phobos said he'd rather be on Mount Olympus, and Deimos said he liked some of it, but not all of it. Do you think he meant me, when he said he didn't like all of it?"

"He probably meant the dung heap."

"I don't know, Cupid. Sometimes I think, if given the choice, he'd rather spend a day with a pile of shit than with me."

Cupid laughed and patted her on the back, but she'd been serious.

CHAPTER SEVEN

Critters

When Ellie and Cupid reached the cluster of trees about a hundred meters west of the homestead, they kicked off their boots and squirmed out of their jeans.

The cattle could be seen further upstream in the northwest pasture beneath another cluster of trees.

"We're not that different, are we?" Cupid said of cattle and people.

"I suppose not."

She pulled off her top, so that she was left in her panties and bra. She'd wait for Cupid to turn around before stripping any further.

"Oh, look. Deimos is coming," Cupid said of his brother, who was walking toward them from the homestead. "I wonder why Phobos isn't with him?"

When Deimos reached them, Ellie enjoyed the way he glanced over her body before saying, "I just got stung by a scorpion. Thought I'd warn you. It stings like hell."

"I'm so sorry," Ellie said, checking out the back of his hand, which was red and swollen. "Where did it happen?"

"In the shack. I left my dirty socks on the floor by my bed yesterday, and when I went to pick them up just now, the little turd stung me."

Ellie bet his feet hurt if he worked all morning without socks.

"The cold water should help," Cupid said.

"We need more clothes," Ellie said. "This is ridiculous."

"I've been praying to Artemis about that very thing," Cupid said.

Deimos kicked off his boots and climbed out of his clothes, even his underwear, apparently unconcerned about who saw. Then he climbed down onto a long flat rock a few feet from the bank.

Ellie blushed and averted her eyes when Cupid caught her staring at his brother. He stepped out of his own under things and joined his brother on the rock. They sat side by side and dangled their legs over the stone edge, into the deeper part of the stream.

"Where's Phobos?" Ellie asked Deimos.

"I think he's already out here. Isn't that him, downstream?"

Ellie squinted. Phobos was floating down toward the southern part of the homestead.

"That looks like fun! Look the other way, guys. I'm about to strip."

Cupid turned, but Deimos stared up at her, refusing to cooperate.

She lifted her brows. "Fine."

She kept her eyes locked on his while she did a strip tease for him. She was pleased when he smiled and shook his head. He didn't seem to hate her as much as Phobos did. She wondered why.

She jumped into the middle of the stream, hoping to splash both boys, but, if she'd been successful, she'd never know, because the current hurled her away. She tried not to panic when she couldn't regain her footing. She paddled with her arms, kicked with her legs, and swallowed a lot of water, as she tried to get back up to the surface. When she finally did manage to get her head out of water and her hair out of her eyes, she glanced back to see the stream had carried her a long way from the boys. It continued to carry her as she struggled to swim to the bank. She kept kicking her feet down, trying to feel for the bottom of the stream, but it was too deep.

As she glanced back at the boys again, to see how far she'd gone, she slammed into something—or someone. It was Phobos. He picked her up by the armpits and helped her to her feet. She could finally touch the bottom, with the water up to her neck.

"Thank you," she said, trying to catch her breath. "I nearly drowned. I told you, water hates me."

Through the clear water, she was reminded that he was naked—naked and aroused. He laughed at her reaction and gave her a once-over. "You're welcome."

Then he did something she wasn't expecting. He pulled her body against his and pressed his mouth to hers.

He sucked at her lips and bit hard. Then he swept his mouth down her neck, went underwater, and bit one of her nipples.

It hurt and felt oh-so-good at the same time. She closed her eyes and moaned as he squeezed her other breast with one hand while he squeezed her bottom with the other. When he lifted his head from the water, she smiled up at him, but he looked angry.

"What's wrong?" she asked.

"What *isn't* wrong?" he said. "There's nothing I can do about this arrow of hate. I've tried to fight it, but I can't."

"I'm sorry, Phobos. I'm sorry this has happened to you. I don't blame you for any of your cruelty towards me. I understand. Truly."

Phobos lifted his arms and brushed the hair from his face, as though trying to figure out what to say to her next. The moment his hands left her body, the current carried her past him.

"Help!" she cried just before water flooded her mouth.

She went underwater again as she kicked and paddled, trying to get to the surface. Then Phobos grabbed her by her hair and caught her in his arms.

"You were about to plow into those rocks," he said as he cradled her. "Can you breathe?"

She coughed up water and nodded. When she could, she said, "Thank you. I didn't realize the current was this strong."

"You do that a lot, don't you—do things without fully understanding what you're getting yourself into?"

"What is that supposed to mean?"

He glanced down at her body. "If you don't know, then you don't deserve to be told. Here's the bank. You can climb out on your own."

He set her on her feet next to flat rocks that jutted out from the bank—like the one Deimos and Cupid were sitting on upstream. As she pulled herself onto them, something long, thin, and black swam out from between them. It opened its big white mouth, showed its huge fangs, and hissed at her. She jumped back and screamed.

Phobos caught her again and said, "Dammit, Ellie! That was close. Those things can kill you!"

"Don't you think I know that?" she hollered. "Anyway, I'm immortal. I keep forgetting."

"You can still die, and it's rarely pleasant."

"Where did it go?"

"It swam away."

"Fuck! That scared the hell out of me! Why would Christina let the girls float down a stream that has water moccasins in it?"

"They don't usually attack people—only when they feel threatened."

"It's not like I threatened it on purpose," she said.

"Don't blame *me*. How was I supposed to know it was hiding in these rocks?"

"I'm *not* blaming you. This was nobody's fault."

His expression was cold, his eyes full of rage.

"What happened to the man who kissed me a few moments ago? I want *that* man back."

He clenched his jaw and set her on her feet near the rocks again. "Be careful what you wish for."

As they were headed across the pea gravel to the farmhouse for lunch, Deimos said to Phobos, "You treat her like shit, and she still chooses you."

"I didn't know we had an audience."

"It was hard to miss."

"Bro', she didn't *choose* me. I took her."

Phobos opened the back door of the farmhouse and gestured for his brother to enter first, letting him think whatever he wished about Phobos's last comment.

Ellie and Cupid were already seated at the family table across from the two little girls with plates of food in front of them. Cupid had met Phobos and Ellie downstream with their clothes, but Phobos hadn't been ready to climb out yet. He'd wanted to finish in private what Ellie had started. Deimos had waited on him at the shack, so they were both a little late.

As Phobos and Deimos sat across from one another at the other table, Christina brought them plates with an open-faced burger and all the trimmings on the side.

"Thank you," Phobos said. "Are these tomatoes from your garden?"

"Yes. The pickles and lettuce, too. I pickle my own cucumbers."

"We raised the beef, too," Danny added as he delivered glasses of tea.

"This looks delicious," Deimos said. "Thank you."

"You're welcome," Christina said, before returning to the kitchen to make her plate. "I was telling Cupid and Ellie that I found a box of clothes left on the front porch for you. Artemis must have come by."

"I was so relieved to have clean jeans to wear!" Ellie said, standing from the bench to show them off.

Phobos liked the way they hugged her ass. *Good job, Artemis.*

"Tell me she brought socks," Deimos said.

"Socks, underwear, jeans, shirts, and even bathing suits," Ellie said.

"And a second pair of boots for each of us," Cupid added.

"Thank the gods," Deimos said. "My feet have blisters from wearing my boots without socks."

Jaquelyn carried a plate from the kitchen and sat in her usual place. Then she grinned at Phobos. "Now that you have swimming trunks, you won't have to walk around the stream, naked as a jaybird."

Rose laughed and repeated, "Naked as a jaybird? What does that mean, Mimi?"

"It means in your birthday suit," Christina said.

"Is it my birthday?" Rose asked.

Everyone laughed.

Danny brought his plate from the kitchen and sat down. "No, *mija.* Your birthday is in February. This is August."

"Oh."

"Do you ever wonder why people don't say *naked as a cow,* or *naked as a horse?*" Phobos asked. "Why the jaybird, of all creatures? They're *all* naked."

"Naked as a pig?" Rose asked, giggling. "Or, naked as an elephant?"

"Exactly! Rose is making my point." Phobos got up and held out his fist to her. "Give me a fist bump, girlfriend."

Rose bumped her tiny fist to his, but said, "I'm not your girlfriend."

Phobos busted out laughing, and so did the others, as he returned to his seat.

Deimos lifted his finger. "Actually, that phrase doesn't refer to birds. It comes from the 1920's and 30's, when prisoners in America came off the bus and were forced to walk from the showers to their cells carrying their kits without clothes on. Prisoners were called jailbirds, or j-birds for short."

"Thank you, Professor Deimos," Phobos said.

Ellie giggled.

"Allow me to apologize for my brothers in advance," Cupid said to the Garcias with a teasing grin. "Like the dung heap, you get used to them after a while."

Rose hit the table with her hand and laughed.

Jaquelyn threw back her head and guffawed.

"You boys are hilarious," Christina said. "I'm glad to have you around."

"Me, too, Mimi," Rose said.

"Me, too, Mimi," Violet, who hadn't said a single word as far as Phobos knew, repeated.

"She talks?" he asked.

"Only when she wants to," Danny said.

"Thanks again for getting those fire ants off of her today," Christina said. "She only got bit in two places. It could have been so much worse."

Violet climbed from her bench.

"Where are you going, *mija*?" Christina asked her.

The little girl didn't answer as she walked up to Phobos. Then she lifted her knee to show him where she'd been stung by an ant.

Phobos showed her the bites on his hand and thumb. "Those mean ants got us, didn't they?"

"Mean ants!" she repeated as she stomped her foot.

Phobos chuckled. She was adorable. Seeing her interact with her family made him wonder if he might, one day, like to have kids. He glanced across the room at Ellie, who was smiling at him.

He immediately filled with rage. Why couldn't he look at her without feeling overwhelmed with hatred? He knew, somewhere deep inside, he still cared for her; otherwise, he wouldn't have helped her today in the stream. Instinct drove him to protect her, yet the arrow compelled him to hate her.

And, sometimes, when Ellie did something to remind him of their days spent together at Cupid's castle, the arrow of love tingled. Phobos fought with all his might to quell the hate and stoke the love.

It was enough to drive a person mad.

After lunch, Danny told them to fill their canteens and put on sunscreen, because they'd be out in the sun for the rest of the day. Once they'd done what he'd said, they helped him pile tools and fencing into the bed of the pickup, and then they headed in the truck toward the south fence.

Ellie jumped out to open and close the gate, and then Danny drove them to the west side of the south fence and parked along the shoulder, where one of the posts was sagging and the wire was no longer taut.

As Danny showed them how to remove and check the post, to see if it was still good, and then how to reset it when it was, Phobos found himself staring at the stream and recalling what had happened there between him and Ellie.

"These wires aren't live right now," Danny was saying. "But come winter, when we move the herd to his pasture, they will be."

They spent the afternoon driving from one post to another, either replacing or resetting it and tightening the wire between it or replacing the wire with some from the roll on the back of the pickup. Mending fences wasn't as bad as shoveling dung, but spending hours beneath the sun without relief was miserable. Phobos continued to ask Helios to move behind some clouds and give them a break. Phobos supposed it wasn't the sun god's fault that there were no clouds in the skies today. He prayed to Iris and asked her to please refill the clouds and send rain.

Phobos also wrestled with the conflicting feelings he had for Ellie. After holding her in his arms, after touching her and kissing her, he'd been reminded of how much he once loved her. Was it possible to love and hate someone at the same time?

When Jaquelyn flirted with him again at lunch, he'd realized something. He'd realized that he'd been using Jaquelyn as a distraction from what he really wanted. It hadn't been fair to either woman. He'd been wrong to lead Jaquelyn on and wasn't sure how to remedy it.

And then there was Deimos. The comment his brother had made to him on the way to lunch haunted Phobos. Did Eris's arrow affect Deimos differently than it had affected Phobos? His brother didn't seem to be filled with rage and hatred. He seemed annoyed with Ellie, but not angry. And his comment before lunch proved that he still wanted Ellie.

Why did that fill Phobos with such profound jealousy?

As they piled the tools back into the bed of the truck and headed back to the homestead, Phobos said a silent prayer to Hera: *Well played, Hera. You've made me more miserable than I ever thought possible.*

CHAPTER EIGHT

Horseback Riding

Ellie had no problem falling asleep that night but found her morning chores after breakfast less of a novelty than she had the previous day. Shoveling dung, spreading hay, and adding more feed to the food bins would get old fast, even if she enjoyed the view of the animals, the land, and the twins working beside her.

She looked forward to grooming the horses. Today, she worked on Gypsy. Brushing her coat and talking softly to Gypsy comforted Ellie as much, if not more, than it did the horse.

Ellie needed that comfort, because the twins were confusing the hell out of her. Just when she'd think they were overcoming the effects of the arrow of hate, Phobos would make a rude comment to her, or Deimos would ignore her.

She was able to bear it all a little better today—including the miserable four hours they spent in the afternoon mending the D.C. fence—because she was looking forward to horseback riding before dusk.

At six o'clock that evening, they met at the stables in the tack room, where Danny showed Ellie and the twins how to saddle and bridle the horses, with help from Cupid and Jaquelyn. Danny also went over safety practices and other horseback riding etiquette. Ellie couldn't wait for him to finish his lecture so they could get started.

"We start at walk, then transition to trot, and finally, to canter," Danny said. "The horses are familiar with these terms, along with *go, slow down,* and *halt.* When you say *go,* they know to walk. They've come to understand that *go* and *walk* are interchangeable. If you want them to trot, say *trot*. For canter, say *canter*. Don't say, *faster*. Got it?"

"What about *gallop*?" Cupid asked.

"Let's not try that on the first day," Danny said.

Ellie was pleased when Danny told her to ride Gypsy, since they'd spent a lot of time together that morning. Jaquelyn had mounted Sherlock by standing on a wooden box, so Ellie did the same, with Cupid's help. Jaquelyn and Sherlock were already waiting in the pen.

"Go ahead and take Gypsy to the pen while the others mount," Danny told Ellie once she had mounted.

Ellie said, "Go, Gypsy," but the horse just stood there.

"She's old and stubborn," Danny said. "Give her a squeeze with your heels and speak to her more forcefully. You have to show her that you're ahead of her in the pecking order, or she won't do anything you say."

Ellie kicked her heels against the horse and commanded, "Go, Gypsy!"

The horse walked from the stables to the pen and went to a corner, near the east homestead fence, and pulled up a clump of tall grass.

"Don't let her feed," Jaquelyn said. "She's trying to assert dominance over you. Pull up on the reins—not too hard."

This was not as easy as Ellie had expected. She hadn't realized she'd have to play the part of a task master to get Gypsy to cooperate.

"Really, Gypsy!" Ellie said in frustration. "I thought we were friends."

"It's not about friendship," Jaquelyn said. "It's about respect. Make her mind you. The sooner the better."

Ellie pulled up on the reins. "Walk, Gypsy!"

Gypsy obeyed. Then Ellie used the reins to guide Gypsy to wait behind Sherlock.

"Halt!"

"There you go," Jaquelyn said.

The brothers came out, one by one, and joined them in the pen. Cupid rode Chestnut, Deimos had Bailey, and Phobos rode Blondie. The sight of the three handsome brothers looking rugged, strong, and masculine as they rode their horses into the pen took Ellie's breath away. Jaquelyn appeared to be equally charmed.

Ellie was pleased when Deimos met her eyes and winked. She couldn't stop the smile from cracking her face in half.

And yet, he confused her more than ever. Just that afternoon, when she'd attempted to tease him about the sunburn on his nose, he'd ignored her. Why was he giving her so many mixed signals?

Danny opened the gate to the pasture. "Don't forget that Chestnut is the alpha. Allow Cupid to ride in front and avoid getting too close to him."

Cupid took Chestnut through the gate and then rode the open pasture at trot. Jaquelyn waited for Phobos and Deimos to go ahead of her. Then Jaquelyn went and signaled to Ellie to come, too.

The horses followed Chestnut, just as Danny had said they would. Cupid took Chestnut to canter, and the others followed. He led them straight across the east pasture, toward the hayfield fence. Ellie loved the feeling of the wind on her face as she and Gypsy took up the rear of the herd. Ellie also enjoyed the view the others ahead of her, especially the view of her favorite twins.

Ellie felt so invigorated by the rush of adrenaline—after hours of boring, monotonous work—that she shouted, "YEE HAW!"

Jaquelyn turned back and gave her a bright smile. Phobos rolled his eyes. The others hadn't seemed to hear.

There weren't many trees in the pasture. Most of them were down by the south fence, where the stream ran from the tank down to the hayfields. Aside from a cluster of trees near the stables, there was a row along the hayfield fence and a cluster in the northeastern corner.

It took about five minutes to get from one side of the pasture to the other. As they approached the trees that lined the hayfield fence, Cupid slowed to trot. The herd followed. Ellie didn't even have to tell Gypsy what to do.

Cupid turned north, uphill, and returned to canter. As they rode along the hayfield fence, Ellie and the others had to occasionally duck to avoid a low-hanging branch. It made the experience more exciting.

A few minutes later, Cupid slowed to trot as he approached the center fence. This time, Ellie had to say, "Trot," to get Gypsy to slow down. Fortunately, Gypsy listened and slowed behind the others.

When Cupid turned Chestnut west, back toward the homestead, he returned to canter, and again the herd followed. After a few minutes, Ellie saw Rusty the bull grazing in the northeast pasture beneath a tree.

"Hi, Rusty!" she shouted as she cantered by.

Because she'd been looking at Rusty, Ellie hadn't noticed that Jaquelyn and the others had slowed to trot, and she and Gypsy passed Sherlock and Blondie to avoid running into them.

Ellie pulled on the reins and shouted, "Gypsy, trot!"

After a few paces at trot, Ellie said, "Walk!"

So much for Gypsy following the herd, Ellie thought as she kicked with her heels and pulled on the reins to get Gypsy back in line with the others. Fortunately, she was listening to Ellie's commands and not ignoring her as she had at first.

"It's okay," Cupid hollered. "We're turning here, anyway. Just wait there until we pass."

Ellie walked Gypsy in a circle as the others headed south at trot. Then she and Gypsy fell in line behind Jaquelyn. They trotted downhill in the evening breeze toward the sparkling stream near the front of the property. Cupid slowed Chestnut to walk, and everyone, including Gypsy, slowed, too.

"Let them drink and rest for a few minutes," Cupid said as the horses moved beside one another at the stream.

Ellie and the others drank from their canteens as the horses drank from the streams.

Because this pasture wasn't as steep as the western pasture, the current was slower here than the one that had nearly drowned Ellie. She decided that next time she would go for a swim, it would be here.

Earlier that day, when they'd had some free time before lunch, she'd slipped into her bathing suit and had planned to take a dip in the northeast pasture, preferring to take her chances with Rusty rather than fight the current in the west pasture. But all three boys had talked her out of it, because they didn't trust Rusty. Cupid had insisted that if she sat on the rocks and avoided the middle of the stream, she'd be fine.

Although he'd been right and she'd been safe on the shallow rocks, it had been boring and awkward for Ellie. She'd just sat there with Cupid and Deimos while Phobos took another ride on the current. Deimos hadn't said two words to her, and Cupid had been too tired to talk.

As she waited for Gypsy to have her drink, Ellie said, "We should swim here tonight, before supper."

"This is my favorite swimming spot," Jaquelyn said.

"You should join us then," Phobos added.

Ellie tried to hide her frustration with Phobos as Jaquelyn said, "Okay."

A few minutes later, Cupid took the lead at walk, back toward the hayfield. The other horses got in line, but Gypsy refused to follow, even after Ellie said, "Walk, Gypsy!"

Instead, the stubborn mare fed on a clump of grass while the others continued to trot, and then canter, away, leaving Ellie behind.

"Gypsy!" Ellie complained.

She struggled for a few minutes, kicking her heels into the sides of the horse, pulling on her reins, and using a forceful voice and then gave up and climbed down, thinking she could manage better on foot.

Deimos trotted up to Ellie on Bailey before slowing to walk. "What are you doing?"

"Gypsy won't listen."

"Halt, Bailey." To Ellie, Deimos said, "Cupid's going to take the others around once more. We can cut down the middle and catch up. Come on."

On foot, Ellie pulled Gypsy by the reins to get her away from the clumps of grass she'd been feeding on. Once she'd got the horse to stop eating, Ellie tried to mount her, but the stirrup was too high for her to get a good footing.

"Cupid should have adjusted those for you," Deimos said as he climbed down from Bailey. "You don't need the stirrups this high with your long legs. They were meant for Christina."

He grabbed Ellie by the waist and helped her up. The feel of his touch sent goosebumps over every inch of her skin, even though it was at least ninety degrees outside.

Once she and Deimos were both mounted, Ellie asked, "Why are you being nice to me?"

Deimos put a finger to his lips, as if to silence her. "I'm not being nice," he said gruffly. "I'm just doing what Cupid told me to do. Come on."

As much as Phobos had enjoyed riding the horses, he was glad when he and the others had removed the tack and turned out the horses, because that meant cooling off in the stream. The heat in southwest Texas in August was nearly intolerable for him. Once his six months were up, Phobos planned to leave and to never look back.

Although he preferred swimming nude, he, along with his brothers, wore the trunks Artemis had sent as a courtesy to the Garcia family, who'd commented one too many times about Phobos strolling around "naked as a j-bird." Ellie had been given a yellow one-piece that looked incredible on her. At first, Phobos had wished he had his x-ray vision. But once Ellie had gone into the water and had gotten the suit wet, he found he didn't need it.

He silently thanked Artemis again for her choice of clothing for Ellie.

Jaquelyn was there in a tiny bikini that left nothing to the imagination, either, because every time she jumped in, the top rolled up over her breasts, and the bottoms went up her ass.

And the water was crystal clear.

So, for the women, the bathing suits were an unnecessary and inauthentic token of modesty.

Phobos could see why this spot was Jaquelyn's favorite. It had the most shade, the best breeze, and a gentle current. It also had a rope tied to a tree branch that hung over the deepest part, and it was fun to climb up the tree and swing from the rope and into the stream.

The first time Phobos had swung from the rope, the feeling of dropping toward the water had terrified him. He was used to his power of flight, and it was unnerving not to have it.

But, as he became accustomed to the feeling, he found he enjoyed the rope. He supposed swinging from it was the closest he'd get to flight until his sentence was over.

He also enjoyed watching Ellie and Cupid compete as they each tried to outdo the other with forward and backward flips and other tricks from the rope. As much hate as Phobos felt for Ellie, his love of competition drove him to get in on the action.

What he didn't enjoy was how Jaquelyn was becoming more assertive with him, now that they were out of her parents' company. He'd enjoyed her flirtations at first. She'd punched his shoulder when he'd made a joke. She'd slapped his bottom while they were waiting in line at the rope. And she'd attempted to dunk him underwater while they were in the deeper part of the stream. But just now, as they rested from their jumping competition, Jaquelyn approached him in waist-deep water, and squeezed his ass.

He didn't want to hurt the girls' feelings, so he laughed it off and said, "Let's not get ahead of ourselves."

Her face flushed bright pink as she took a step back. "Sorry. I thought you'd like that."

Phobos glanced at Ellie, who was sitting on a rock across the bank talking to Deimos. They were sitting close and speaking quietly together, as if exchanging something private. Phobos was filled with jealousy and rage.

Jaquelyn noticed. "Oh. Are you into Ellie? I thought…"

He cupped Jaquelyn's face and pressed his mouth hard against hers. He closed his eyes, and, in his mind, he was kissing Ellie. The confusion of love, anger, and lust drove him wild.

He quickly pulled away from the girl and apologized. He hadn't meant to use her.

"It's okay," she said. "I liked it."

Phobos glanced across the stream and was glad that Ellie and Deimos were staring at him with looks of disapproval, because that meant they'd seen. Let them be angry at him, he thought. He had enough anger to go around.

"Listen," Jaquelyn said. "There's a county dance this weekend about an hour's drive from here. It's called Night in Ol' Del Rio."

"A county dance?" he repeated, not sure what that meant.

"They have food and beer booths, live bands, and a big dancefloor, and there's a carnival, too, with games and rides. My family goes every year on Saturday night. It's kind of a tradition. We're hoping y'all will go with us this year."

"Did you hear that?" Phobos shouted to Ellie and his brothers. "We're going to a dance and carnival this weekend!"

CHAPTER NINE

Mixed Messages

That night at supper, as they ate venison chili with pinto beans and cornbread, the family talked more about their tradition of going to Night in Ol' Del Rio, which was always held on the second weekend of August.

But Ellie was only half-listening, because she was preoccupied with the conversation she'd had earlier with Deimos.

As they'd sat beside one another at the swimming spot watching Cupid swing from the rope, she'd asked him if there was something that he wasn't telling her.

"Not now," he'd muttered.

"Why not?"

"We're being watched."

She'd understood what he'd meant: There was something he wanted to tell her, but he didn't want the other gods to overhear.

"Can you write it?" she'd whispered.

"In code. Later. Now stop."

That was about the time they'd noticed Phobos kiss Jaquelyn. It had made Ellie sick to her stomach. She hadn't blamed Jaquelyn. She was a nice girl, and Ellie liked her.

But yesterday, after the stream that had nearly drowned her had slammed her into him, Phobos had given Ellie the impression that he was fighting against the arrow of hate. She'd come to believe that he was fighting for *her*. And that belief had made his rude comments bearable. She'd come to respect the struggle going on inside of him.

Kissing Jaquelyn had sent a different message. If Phobos wanted Ellie to feel as much hate for him as the arrow made him feel for her, well, congratulations—she wanted to say—you did it.

Yet, she supposed she had no right to be angry at Phobos for flirting with another girl when Ellie had been unable to choose between him and his brother. She was a hypocrite for wanting his undivided love and loyalty when she was unable to give him hers.

Ellie rejoined the conversation at supper when Deimos asked Christina if he could borrow a pen, some paper, and a hole punch—if she had one.

"I don't have a hole punch," Christina said. "But I'll get you the pen and paper."

"I have one," Jaquelyn said, jumping from her chair. "I needed it for school last year, for my binder. I'll grab it for you."

Deimos avoided Ellie's gaze, which confirmed, in her mind, that his request had something to do with the coded message he planned to give her.

What if the arrow of hate hadn't worked on him, and he wanted to tell her that he still loved her? This thought lifted Ellie to the moon, despite how hurt she felt over Phobos kissing Jaquelyn. Maybe this was a sign that she was meant to let Phobos go and choose Deimos.

Ellie was tired that night but had a hard time falling asleep, because she couldn't stop thinking about what Deimos might tell her. She dared not pray to the gods about it, because it was important that they never know her suspicions. If they thought the arrow of hate hadn't worked on Deimos, they would separate them, sending one of them someplace else to carry out the rest of the sentence, and that could be much worse than their current situation.

As she lay there on the bottom bunk, listening to Cupid snore, she glanced through the window near her bed to gaze at the stars, but searching for constellations didn't help her fall asleep.

She turned over and was startled when Deimos entered her room. He was about to tuck his folded papers beneath her pillow when he saw she was awake. She smiled up at him and took his folded message, eager to read its contents. Before he left, she climbed from her bunk and wrapped her arms around his neck, tucking her face against his throat.

"Thank you," she whispered against his skin, breathing in his scent.

She missed being in his arms. She longed for him to hold her as he once did.

"I love you," she whispered.

When she released him, he had a funny look on his face, as though she'd confused him.

He handed her the flashlight and left her room without explanation.

She climbed back in bed and unfolded the papers before shining the flashlight on the first page. It read:

The art of horseback riding, introduced by our very own Athena after Poseidon created the first horse, requires much patience and hard work. I hope you have realized after today's failure that you will need to improve your performance if you don't wish the ranchers to ever throw you out.

She read it again, finding it an oddly written note, but unable to discern any code in it. Then she looked at the second paper. It was full of holes. She immediately realized she was to use the second paper as a cipher to read the first.

She carefully lined up the pages and read the message that appeared through the holes:

The arrow of hate neutralized love. I don't hate you.

She immediately tore up the cipher, lest one of the gods happened to notice her reading with it. She tore it into several tiny pieces, taking out her frustration with each rip. Her hopes had been dashed. She'd been expecting a profession of love; instead, Deimos had merely conveyed that he didn't hate her.

"Ellie?" Cupid asked from the top bunk. "Is that you?"

"Yes. I'm sorry. Go back to sleep."

She quietly folded the handwritten message and tucked it beneath her pillow.

Then she turned onto her stomach and gazed out the window at the stars on the horizon.

Sometime later, she heard a noise outside her window. Thinking it must be Julio or Iglesias, she wasn't concerned. Then Phobos was standing there, wearing nothing but his white briefs. His underwear did nothing to hide the fact that he was aroused.

Why had he come to her window, especially if he was into Jaquelyn?

Ellie couldn't tell if he knew she was awake as he slipped his hand beneath the waistband, because he was staring at her bottom.

After he'd gone on for a minute or more, she closed her eyes, pretending to be asleep, and rolled onto her back. Then she lifted her shirt over her breasts and rubbed them, pinching her nipples until they were hard—all the while pretending like she was having an erotic dream. Then she slipped her panties down and stroked herself.

His gasp let her know he was watching.

She smiled and opened her eyes, just in time to see him climax. He was startled to discover she'd been awake. The look on his face made her laugh out loud. She quickly covered her mouth, so as not to wake Cupid. Phobos furrowed his brows, his face full of hate and resentment, and left the window. She heard the wooden boards creak beneath him as he came back inside and headed to his room. She looked up through the door to the hall. He glanced at her, balled his fists, and returned to his bed.

She pulled her up her panties and pushed down her shirt and tried once again to go to sleep, but she was too upset. She'd been hoping for a smile or some sign of love and tenderness from Phobos.

Two strikes in one night was too much to bear.

Phobos got little sleep after Ellie had humiliated him by laughing at him. He supposed it was his punishment for kissing Jaquelyn. Maybe he deserved it. But it did nothing to help him in his battle against the hate.

Over the next few days, he found it more and more difficult to interact with the women on the ranch. He suspected Christina was aware that something was going on between him and her daughter, because she wasn't as friendly toward him as she'd been after he'd helped Violet with the ants.

Jaquelyn was distant with him in front of her family, but whenever her parents weren't around, she expected his undivided attention. To get more of it, she'd begun showing up at the swimming spot every day before lunch and in the evenings, before dusk.

He'd begun to look forward to it less and less.

He wanted to be interested in Jaquelyn. At times, he tried to give it a chance. And he supposed that only made things worse, because he was sending her mixed signals.

But he couldn't get Ellie out of his heart. It felt as if the arrow of hate and the arrow of love were side by side, compelling him in opposite directions. Instead of neutralizing one another, they overwhelmed him with conflicting desires. He wanted to hurt her and to protect her, to take pleasure from her and to give it, to rage at her and to caress her in equal measure.

When Ellie spoke sweetly to the little girls or to the animals, when she told a funny joke at mealtime, when she laughed out loud at one of *his* jokes, or when she did a daring jump from the rope swing, the impulse to love won out. And when she doted over Deimos's scorpion sting, or sat near Deimos in the stream, or glanced at Deimos with a look of affection, the impulse to hate raged through every fiber of his being.

Phobos recognized that he'd contributed to Ellie's growing dependence on Deimos by starting something with Jaquelyn. If Phobos had listened to his brother and had backed off the rancher's daughter, the arrow of love might have had a fighting chance.

This made Phobos resent Jaquelyn, even though she wasn't to blame. He was further infuriated that Ellie and Jaquelyn had become friends. It angered him, because it suggested that Ellie was moving on. She'd given up on their love, after less than a week.

Saturday afternoon, they finished the last of the fence work early and were given the rest of the day off, with the expectation that they'd join the Garcia family that evening after supper at Night in Ol' Del Rio.

After a quick dip in the swimming spot with the others, Phobos left early to get some much-needed sleep. When he awoke an hour or so later, he heard giggling. He went outside to find Cupid, Deimos, and Ellie still in their swimming suits washing near the well. Deimos sat on one of the chairs from the shack, under a tree between the well and the west homestead fence. His hair was lathered in shampoo, and the lower half of his face was covered in shaving cream. Ellie stood over him with a razor, giggling. Cupid sat nearby on the stone ledge that surrounded the well. He looked newly washed and shaved and was giggling, too.

"I never knew you were so ticklish, Deimos," Ellie was saying. "Now hold still, or you might get cut."

"Hey, Phobos," Cupid said when he noticed his brother. "Ellie gave me a shave, and I convinced Deimos to have one, too. It comes with a shampoo, if you're interested."

Phobos scratched at the beard that had been growing on his face since the day he'd arrived.

"I hadn't noticed you'd grown whiskers," he said to Cupid. "Couldn't you just pluck the few hairs and be done with it?"

"Very funny. I had a few more this time. I suppose the Texas heat promotes beard growth."

"Actually," Deimos began, "most people—and animals, too—grow hair and beards more quickly in the summertime. You would think we would have evolved to grow it faster during winter, but that's not what happened."

"Hold still, Professor Deimos," Ellie teased. "And remember, I wanted you to keep your beard. You're the one that asked to have it shaved."

"It's too damn hot for a beard," Deimos said.

"Lean your head back," Ellie said to Deimos.

Ellie dipped a plastic cup into the tub, which was filled with water from the well. She poured the water over the back of Deimos's head as she ran her fingers through his hair, to rinse out the shampoo. Then she dipped one corner of a towel into the tub and used it to wipe the remaining cream from Deimos's face.

"There," she said. "How does that feel? Better?"

Deimos rubbed his chin and nodded. "Much. Thanks."

"Don't forget," Ellie warned. "You owe me a dance."

"That's the price of a shave and shampoo," Cupid said to Phobos. "We have to dance with her at Night in Ol' Del Rio tonight."

"But I'll do you, for free," she said to Phobos. "If you want me to. I wouldn't want to make Jaquelyn mad."

Phobos clenched his jaw in anger. Just when he thought he was managing the rage, she had to make a comment to set him off again.

"I don't need any special favors," he said, trying not to grit his teeth. "I'll pay the same price as everyone else."

He took Deimos's place in the chair and gazed up at Ellie. She was frowning, and it angered him that her playful mood had disappeared with his arrival. If he could pull the arrow of hate from his heart and change things, he would; but he was helpless against it.

Ellie dipped the plastic cup into the bin full of water. "Lean your head back."

He lifted his chin and enjoyed the sensation of her face close to his, as she poured the cold water over his hair. She bent over him, lathering in shampoo and massaging the back of his head. From this point of view, he could see the tops of her breasts dangling over him as she worked. He closed his eyes and nearly purred when she ran her fingernails over his scalp.

"I'm glad you like that," she said softly.

When he looked at her smiling down at him, the rage evaporated, leaving only love and desire.

"Ellie," he said gently.

She stopped massaging. "What is it?"

"I didn't mean to hurt you with Jaquelyn. It was a mistake."

"Are you going to hurt *her* now, too?"

"What choice do I have?"

"There's always a choice."

Rage filled his heart. He knocked her hands away from his head and got up from the chair.

"Don't you want your shave?" she asked.

"Never mind." He took the cup she'd been using and rinsed the shampoo from his head as he bent forward. Then he grabbed a towel from the clothesline and went to the shack to lie down and stew.

CHAPTER TEN

Night in Ol' Del Rio

The fairgrounds on the outskirts of Del Rio were packed with cars on Saturday night, when Danny pulled into the gravel lot to look for a parking place for his truck, a few minutes before nine o'clock. Because they couldn't fit into one vehicle, Christina followed with Jaquelyn and the girls in her black Jetta.

The air was hot and sticky and full of dust, as they walked from the parking lot toward the carnival grounds. Rose and Violet each held onto one of Christina's hands and were asking for cotton candy before they'd entered the gate.

Excited by the strings of colorful lights, crowds of people, and booths of food and games, Ellie didn't mind the sweat accumulating on her face and neck but was glad for the strapless white top, short red skirt, and sandals Jaquelyn had loaned her. Ellie would have been miserable in jeans, though the boys and most of the other people in attendance were wearing them.

"Anybody else want cotton candy?" Christina asked as the girls dragged her toward the cotton candy booth.

The others shook their heads.

"Thanks, anyway," Ellie said. "I'm still full from your delicious chicken-fried steak."

"We'll see you later, then," she said. "We're headed for the kiddie rides."

"Dad, can we have money to play a game?" Jaquelyn asked.

"Money doesn't grow on trees, Jackie Chan," he said affectionately. "Don't you have any birthday money left?"

"Yes, but do I have to use my own money?"

"Why shouldn't you?" Danny asked with a laugh.

Jaquelyn sighed. "Come on guys. Want to watch?"

Ellie and the others followed Jaquelyn through the crowd and down the aisle between the game booths.

"Look at those cute sloth stuffed animals!" Jaquelyn said. "Phobos, do you think you could win me one?"

Ellie watched Phobos's face for signs of how he was feeling tonight, especially about Jaquelyn.

"You'd be better off asking Ellie," Phobos said. "She's the softball pitcher."

"That's right!" Jaquelyn said. "Ellie, please? I really want one of those sloths!"

"I bet you could find it for sale online more cheaply than it costs to play the game," Ellie said.

"She's right," Danny said.

Cupid clapped Ellie on the back. "That's no fun. Come on, Ellie. Show us what you're made of."

"Please, Ellie?" Jaquelyn said again.

When Ellie glanced at Deimos, he shrugged. "Go for it."

Always up for a challenge, Ellie agreed.

They stood in line, waiting for their turn, and watched three men and an older woman throw softballs toward a hole near the back of the booth and miss.

When it was their turn, Jaquelyn gave the booth attendant five dollars, and he handed over three softballs. Jaquelyn gave one to Ellie and held onto the others. Ellie needed to throw all three balls through the hole to win the sloth.

"I haven't thrown a ball in two months," she said as she sized up the distance between her and the hole.

Phobos cocked his head to the side. "That's not true."

"He's right," Cupid said. "I remember it all too well."

Ellie giggled at the memory of playing softball with the celebrities Phobos had rounded up, as a special gift to her.

Jaquelyn's cheeks turned pink, and her smile faded. "Did y'all play on a team together?"

"They played against each other," Deimos said.

"Who won?" Jaquelyn asked.

Phobos chuckled. "I don't recall. Do you, Ellie?"

"I'm pretty sure it was *my* team," she teased.

"Hey, look! It's Ellie Beaufort!" A girl around Jaquelyn's age ran up to Ellie. She was holding hands with another girl about the same age, and both wore ponytails pulled through the back of their baseball caps. "I thought I read that you were taking a year off to tour Europe."

"I am," Ellie said. "I just came to Texas to take care of something, and then I'm headed back."

"Europe?" Jaquelyn repeated. "Wow! I didn't know that."

"Why aren't you playing for the Seminoles again next year—or for any team?" the other girl asked.

Ellie glanced at Deimos and Phobos. "It's a long story."

"Back up and let Ellie throw," Deimos said to the girls.

A crowd had gathered around the booth. Ellie heard her name being murmured by others who recognized her. She wished she'd had a chance to warm up, because she hated letting people down, and she could feel everyone in the crowd depending on her to win the sloth.

She couldn't decide whether she wanted to throw the ball overhand or underhand. She tossed the softball from one hand to the other as she took several paces back.

"Here goes nothing," she muttered beneath her breath.

She threw the ball underhand toward the hole at the back of the booth. The ball shot straight through the hole.

The crowd applauded. Several people—including Danny and Jaquelyn—gave her fist bumps and high fives.

Jaquelyn handed her the second ball. Ellie tried to commit to memory the motion and speed she'd just used. Then she took a few paces back, threw the ball underhand, and it went straight through the hole again.

The cheers were even louder, as more people had gathered to watch the famous Seminoles pitcher try to win a carnival game.

Jaquelyn handed her the third ball. "Good luck!"

Ellie glanced at Deimos and Phobos.

"You've got this," Deimos said.

Phobos gave her a reassuring wink.

She squeezed the ball, remembering the motion and speed. She took a few paces back and sucked in her lips. Then she threw the ball underhand toward the hole. It went straight through for the third time.

The crowd around her erupted with cheers and applause as the sloth was handed to Ellie, who then gave it to Jaquelyn. Jaquelyn hugged Ellie and waved to the crowd, basking in the attention.

As Ellie stepped away from the booth, an old man handed her a longneck bottle of beer. "You earned this, young lady."

"Thank you," Ellie said, accepting the beer.

The longneck bottle was ice cold. She put it to her mouth and drank down the goodness.

Before too long, another man brought her one—and then another. By the time they'd walked from the carnival grounds to where the live band was performing, Ellie had been given eight bottles of beer from fans, which she shared with the group. Because Danny refused, insisting that he buy his own, and because Jaquelyn was underage, there were two bottles each for her and the brothers.

Danny chose a table on the edge of the dancefloor. There were enough chairs for eight people, so they sat and saved the other two for Christina and the girls.

After she'd finished her second beer, Ellie turned to Cupid and Deimos. "You both owe me a dance. Who's going first?"

Cupid and Deimos exchanged glances.

"I don't know how to dance the two-step," Deimos said.

"Come on, then." Cupid offered Ellie his hand.

Smiling from ear to ear, mainly because of the buzz from the beer, Ellie followed Cupid out to the middle of the floor and tried her best to follow his lead as he wrapped one hand around her waist and held the other out to the side.

"I'm not used to this country stuff," she said. "But I thought I'd give it a try."

Cupid laughed. "I'll go easy on you. Just remember this: slow-two, slow-two, quick-quick. Slow-two, slow-two, quick-quick."

"That ain't hard at all," she said. "Oh, my gods, we're doing it."

Even though it had only been two bottles, she already felt drunk, because she rarely drank. Cupid looked drunk, too, occasionally teetering as he guided her across the floor.

"Look at us!" she hollered over Cupid's shoulder to the table where Danny and the others were sitting. "We're doing it!"

Some of the people sitting at other tables lifted their bottles of beer and shouted, "Cheers!" whenever she and Cupid danced by.

"You have a lot of fans here," Cupid said.

"I hope this doesn't get back to my Mama. I don't know what she'll do."

Cupid frowned.

"What's wrong? Did I step on your toe?"

"No. I miss my wife."

"I'm sorry."

"I pray to her constantly, asking for a sign that she forgives me, begging for a visit. Nothing."

"It's only been a week. Give her time."

"You know why she's mad at me, don't you?"

"Because you got your brothers in trouble?"

"No! That's not it at all. She was glad I shot them with arrows of love."

Ellie lifted her brows. "Really?"

"Really."

"Then why is she mad at you?"

"Because when Zeus found out I'd lied to him about Circe, I offered to find you and kill you to save my own skin."

Ellie stopped dancing and stared at Cupid in horror. She'd thought he was her friend. She couldn't believe he could so easily betray her like that.

"You have nothing to fear from me," he said. "I'd never harm you now."

"How am I supposed to believe that? How am I supposed to believe anything you say?"

She stumbled off the dance floor and fled into the crowd.

Phobos saw Ellie run from Cupid's arms in the opposite direction from where he and their group were sitting. For once, he felt in control of his emotions. The alcohol, which had only affected him as a god when he'd consumed large quantities, had numbed his senses, making him feel strangely liberated from the power of the two arrows penetrating his heart.

"Where's Ellie going?" he asked when Cupid returned to the table alone.

"To get some air, I guess." Cupid sat beside Danny, across from Deimos.

Deimos stood. "I need to use the toilet."

"I'll go with you," Phobos said.

As he followed his brother through the crowd, he scanned the faces for Ellie. He wanted her to know how he *really* felt, which he'd only discovered with any certainty moments ago.

He *wanted* her. He was falling in love with her—if he hadn't already. His feelings were real, and it was a relief to know that they were real. As soon as he had the chance, he would tell her.

"Are you okay?" he asked Deimos, who was staggering as he walked.

"Slightly drunk, I think."

"Weird, isn't it? Two beers. I feel the same way. But unlike you, I can walk just fine. I guess we finally know who the superior twin is, don't we?"

"I believe we've always known that, brother," Deimos said, pointing to his brain.

"A vat of useless facts does not a superior make," Phobos teased.

"Now say that fast, five times in a row, and I might believe it."

Phobos laughed as he put an arm around his brother's neck and walked beside him. "I love ya, man."

"That's the alcohol talking, bro'."

"For once, I think it's me."

"I get that. It's numbing the arrows, isn't it?"

"Yes, sir, indeed."

Deimos stopped in his tracks. "There she is! Ellie!"

The sudden stop in momentum made them lose their balance for a moment. Phobos clung to his brother while the world spun a few times and stopped.

Ellie turned and looked at them with tears streaming down her cheeks.

"Don't cry, Ellie," Phobos said as he and his brother hobbled over to her.

She'd been leaning against a rail surrounding the carousel, watching Rose and Violet ride. Christina was standing on the opposite side, waving at her grandchildren as they went by.

Phobos put a hand on Ellie's shoulder, partly to keep his balance. "What happened?"

"Cupid hurt me so bad," she said through tears. "I can't believe he was ready to kill me to save himself on Mount Olympus."

"Oh." Deimos opened his palms toward the sky. "How did you find out?"

"He told me."

Phobos turned to Deimos. "He told her?"

Deimos touched the tip of Ellie's nose. "Why do you suppose he did that?"

Ellie shrugged.

"It was an attempt at an apology. I'm sure of it." Deimos lifted his index finger and staggered back a little until Phobos helped him to regain his balance. "He was desperate when he said it, and I highly doubt he would have gone through with it—not with all he'd already done to protect you. Right? Am I right? Listen to Professor Deimos."

"Then why is Psyche mad at him?" Ellie asked. "And are you *drunk*?"

"I don't know and yes, I think so," Deimos said.

"That makes two of us," Phobos added. "We're not used to alcohol without powers, I guess. But it's a good thing. You want to know why?"

Ellie smiled. "Why?"

He loved that smile. Phobos wanted nothing more than to kiss that smile.

Deimos held Ellie's shoulders. "You know how I said what I said in my letter?"

Ellie nodded.

"This is me, not anything else, okay?" he said.

"Okay."

Then Deimos mouthed, "I love you, too."

Ellie's face transformed. First her beautiful mouth fell open, and then its corners lifted into another gorgeous, sweet smile.

Phobos had meant to tell her the same thing. Now, that plan seemed less valiant. He'd merely be echoing something someone else had already professed. Deimos had beat him to the punch.

And he didn't want to ruin the moment for Deimos.

As Ellie threw her arms around his brother's neck, Phobos backed away and gradually found his way to the table, where Cupid, Danny, and Jaquelyn were sitting.

The band on stage was playing a lively, fast tune. In fact, he believed it was a song by Juicy Jenkins, which reminded him of better days.

"Want to dance?" Phobos asked Jaquelyn.

She glanced at her father, who shrugged.

"Sure!" she said as she popped up out of her chair. "Let's go!"

C H A P T E R   E L E V E N

The Helm of Invisibility

As Deimos swayed with her in his arms on the dancefloor, Ellie whispered in his ear, "I'm in heaven."

"Sshh." He spat. "Careful. Okay?"

"Okay."

Ellie felt like she was dreaming. She stroked his cheek, smooth from the shave she'd given him earlier. Then she ran her fingers through his dark red hair.

"That feels nice," he said, closing his eyes for a moment.

"I want to kiss you so badly," she said.

"Careful," he reminded her.

She wondered if he was being overly cautious. Didn't the other gods have more important concerns than making sure she and the twins suffered?

"I'm not convinced this is necessary," she said.

"I don't want to risk it. Do you?"

"I suppose not."

"Remember when I showed you one of the most important objects in the world?"

She nodded. He was referring to the helm of invisibility.

"I wish I had it now."

She giggled. "I'd give anything to have it."

She said a prayer saying as much to Hades.

"It makes you think, though, doesn't it?" he said a few moments later.

"What?"

"Two people were shot. Two different reactions. Makes you wonder if it's because their real feelings were different."

She knew what he was trying to say without saying it. He was suggesting that he was less affected by the arrow of hate because his feelings of love had been genuine.

As happy as it made her to know that Deimos still loved her, it hurt to think that Phobos didn't and possibly never had. Even now, she loved them both. Maybe this was the Fates' way of forcing her to choose.

She glanced at Phobos across the dancefloor, where he was holding Jaquelyn in his arms. Why couldn't Ellie be happy? Wouldn't they all be better off if she chose Deimos? Phobos seemed to be no longer interested, anyway.

When the song ended, Deimos led her back to their table, where Christina held a sleeping Violet. Rose sat beside them and appeared to be fighting sleep.

"Ready to go?" Danny asked as Phobos and Jaquelyn caught up to them. "Dawn will come early tomorrow."

"And my arms are tired," Christina added.

They all left the dance area and headed through the carnival to the gravel lot. Ellie slipped into the back seat between Cupid and Deimos before Phobos could complain. She enjoyed the excuse to be close to Deimos without worrying that a spy might discover their secret.

As Ellie was returning to the shack for bed after using the bathroom in the farmhouse, she was startled by the appearance of Hecate standing beside the well with her finger to her lips.

She was holding the helm of invisibility.

Hecate took her hand, placed the helm on Ellie's head, and vanished.

Elated, Ellie prayed to Hecate—and to Hades, who must have condoned the gift—with her gratitude. As she did, she carefully crept over the pea gravel and tip-toed into the shack. The boys were already lying in their bunks. At least one of them was snoring. She tip-toed toward Deimos and Phobos's room. When a floorboard creaked beneath her, she held still for a few seconds before moving on.

First, she gazed down at Phobos, who lay with his eyes closed in the bottom bunk. He looked handsome in his beard, even with his brows knitted together, as though he were having a bad dream. She wished she could reach down and smooth his forehead and make his anger disappear. Instead, she bit her lip and told herself to get over it.

She reached up to the top bunk and touched Deimos's arm. At first, he didn't move. Then she caressed him until he opened his eyes. She put one finger to her lips, as Hecate had done, and pointed to the helm.

"How?"

She put her finger to *his* lips and beckoned him to follow her.

Deimos climbed from his bunk, wearing nothing but a pair of briefs. Once they were outside beneath the moonlight, she took his hand, to share the protection of the helm with him.

He slid his arms around her waist and pulled her close as he smiled down at her. She ran her hands across his magnificent chest and abs. Then he gently touched his lips to hers.

Resisting the urge to purr and moan, she raked her fingers through his vibrant hair as he caressed her lips with his. He licked her neck and nibbled her ear before stroking her lips with his again.

She'd missed his gentle kisses and slow caresses—not that she didn't ignite beneath Phobos's hard and frenzied ones. But Deimos knew how to build up her anticipation, so that she was absolutely aching for him to touch her.

At last, he slid his hands from her waist to her bottom. She gasped when he squeezed her there before lifting her up. She wrapped her legs around his waist as he carried her across the pea gravel to the stables, where he set her down on her feet again.

He'd been smart to take her there, because they could be silent on the concrete aisle, unlike the pea gravel. Not wanting to step on his toes, she kicked off her boots. He pulled her body into his and kissed her and kissed her. His hands caressed her back beneath her t-shirt before reaching below her jeans and panties to grab and squeeze her bottom again. He pressed her hard against him. Not wanting anything between them, she lifted her t-shirt over her head—carefully, so as not to knock off the helm—and dropped it at her feet. His hands kneaded her breasts, and she had to bite her tongue to prevent herself from gasping out loud when his mouth found one of her nipples.

He pushed her jeans and panties down to the floor and helped her to step out of them. When he stroked her between the legs, she covered her mouth, to stifle her gasp. Then he stepped out of his briefs, cupped his hands around her bottom, and lifted her again.

She sucked in her lips to keep from crying out as they climaxed together. Then he carefully lowered them to the floor, where they lay side by side on the cool concrete. He made a pillow for himself out of her t-shirt and jeans, and she used his bicep for her own. They lay there together, enjoying the feel of being in each other's arms.

When the dinner bell rang before dawn, Phobos groaned. His head hurt and he wanted more sleep. He rolled over, deciding to wait until he heard Deimos get out of bed.

"Phobos!" Cupid called.

"Huh?" He looked up at his brother, wondering how much time had passed since he'd heard the dinner bell.

"Ellie and Deimos have gone to breakfast without us. We're late. Come on."

Phobos slipped into his jeans and a t-shirt and pulled on his boots, complaining to his parents, like he did nearly every morning, for doing nothing to alleviate his misery.

He was surprised when he entered the farmhouse to find that Ellie and Deimos weren't there.

"Morning," Jaquelyn said cheerfully as she handed him a plate of biscuits, gravy, eggs, and sausage.

"Morning. Is Deimos in the bathroom?" he asked.

"We haven't seen him yet this morning," Danny said as he handed Phobos and Cupid mugs of coffee. "They weren't in their bunks?"

Cupid gave Deimos a look of alarm. "No."

"Maybe they're rinsing off at one of the streams," Christina said. "I can't wait to get the smell of cigarette smoke out of *my* hair and skin."

Phobos took a sip of the coffee. He doubted they'd go in the dark. "I'll go check."

He carried the mug with him as he walked across the pea gravel.

"Deimos? Ellie?" he called out.

He went past the well and the shack toward the barn. "Deimos? Ellie?"

Deimos emerged from the stables in his bare feet, wearing nothing more than his briefs.

"Hey, Phobos." He was grinning from ear to ear.

Had he been in the stables with Ellie all night? Phobos felt the rage flow through him. "Where've you been?"

"I woke up in the stables. I must have walked out there in my sleep last night. I guess it was the alcohol."

Phobos narrowed his eyes. "Where's Ellie?"

"How should I know?"

"Because she's missing, too."

"Did I hear someone say my name?" Ellie said as she emerged from the shack, wearing her work clothes and boots.

Phobos scratched his head. "You weren't in your bunk this morning."

"I was in the outhouse. I had to go before Jaquelyn rang the bell. I didn't know what time it was."

"You were in there for a long time."

"So? I was constipated. Jeez Louise."

Phobos didn't believe her. She and Deimos had been together. Did they really think they could hide it from him?

It wasn't the last time Phobos suspected that Ellie and Deimos were sneaking off together.

Over the next couple of weeks, they irritated the hell out of him. They ignored one another at mealtimes and rarely spoke while they shoveled dung, spread hay, and groomed horses. But Phobos saw the surreptitious glances they exchanged at the swimming spot and the way Deimos watched out for her when they exercised the horses.

One afternoon, while Phobos and Cupid were in the tractor cutting hay, and Deimos and Ellie helped Danny load dung for some buyers, Phobos asked Cupid if he'd noticed anything strange about their behavior.

"It's not something I want to talk about," Cupid said.

"So, you *have* noticed?"

Cupid shrugged.

A few days later, while he and Ellie were in the tractor together raking the hayfields, to get the hay ready for baling, he said, "I know what's going on between you and Deimos."

Her eyes widened, and her mouth dropped open. It was too late for her to deny it.

Then she said, "If you care for your brother, you won't say another word about it."

A mixture of heartache and rage took possession of him, and he bore it as best as he could.

The following Sunday afternoon, they were invited to float on inner-tubes down the stream in the west pasture with Christina, Jaquelyn, and the little ones. Phobos was in no mood, but when Rose pleaded with him and then resorted to calling him a scaredy cat, he gave in.

Still angry with Deimos and Ellie, he focused his attention on the little ones and managed to have some light-hearted fun at first. But the chemistry between his twin brother and Ellie ate him up inside and left him seething.

One night, near the end of August, Phobos awakened to the sound of Deimos climbing from the top bunk. At first, Phobos assumed he was going out for a piss, as he often did in the middle of the night.

But as he closed his eyes, Phobos heard someone else follow Deimos from the shack. Either Cupid was joining him for a piss, or Ellie was sneaking off with him again. He turned in his bed and looked across the hall. Ellie was not in her bed.

As silently as a panther, Phobos crept from the shack in his bare feet to follow them.

Outside, in the moonlight, the homestead was quiet until Phobos stepped onto the pea gravel. His footsteps were accompanied by the chirps of crickets and the leaves blowing in the breeze, but nothing more. And other than the chickens asleep in their coop, there wasn't a soul in sight.

Phobos returned to the shack to make sure he hadn't been dreaming, only to find that Deimos and Ellie were, indeed, gone from their beds. He grabbed the flashlight and went looking for them.

The first place he'd look was the stables.

Before entering, he stood listening for a moment in the dark, with the flashlight off. At first, he heard nothing and was about to search the main barn; but then, he heard the smack of lips locked in a kiss.

Quietly, he pulled the door to the tack room open and stole inside. He kept the flashlight off, not wanting to be seen. He wanted to catch them in the act without them knowing. He had no desire to humiliate his brother.

As he crept into the aisle, he found it empty. He peeked over the doors to each of the stalls and saw no one. He was about to leave, when his foot landed on cloth. In the light of his flashlight, lay a pair of panties. He picked them up and studied them. They were *Ellie's* panties.

He was livid.

He carried the panties back to the shack and threw them on her bed. When she'd return later, she'd wonder how they got there. She'd know that someone knew her secret.

Good. Let her stew on it.

He climbed into bed and tried to sleep, but it was impossible. He lay there for hours, haunted by images of Ellie and Deimos making love all over the ranch. He saw them in the stables, in the barn, in the tractor, at the swimming spot, and even out in the middle of the empty hayfield.

He lay there praying to his parents and to Zeus to end his misery. He wanted to come home. He'd do anything to return to Mount Olympus.

Tears of anger and heartache filled his eyes. Before he could wipe them from his face, he heard the floorboards creak, and he lay very still.

With his face partially hidden by his pillow, he watched for them. He heard them enter his room. He blinked because he couldn't see them. Was he dreaming? Hallucinating? He heard Deimos climb to the top bunk. He heard the smack of a kiss. Then the floorboards creaked under the weight of someone walking to Ellie's bed. He could still hear Deimos shifting above him.

As he stared across the hall at Ellie's bed, he nearly gasped out loud. Where Ellie wasn't, she suddenly was. He didn't see her climb into bed. She was simply gone one moment and there the next.

Unless he was dreaming, that could only mean one thing: Ellie had the helm of invisibility.

CHAPTER TWELVE

A Labor Day Picnic

Ellie was relieved when the last of the haybales had been stacked into the haybarn. Although she'd enjoyed riding in the tractor with Deimos—whether they were cutting, tedding, windrowing, or baling—stacking had been hard work, because they'd had to do it by hand.

She was especially glad because the Garcias always celebrated the end of hay-cutting on the first Monday of September with a Labor Day picnic with all their relatives. And this year, because they had Ellie with them, they wanted to organize a softball game—though it had been agreed upon by the relatives that Ellie wouldn't be allowed to pitch, and there would be a coin toss to determine which team she'd play on. Rose was expecting to play, too, because Ellie had been teaching her how to hit, catch, and throw on Sunday afternoons, when the Garcias returned from church.

It had become a habit for them to go out into the east pasture to play. Danny had even bought a t-ball stand and glove for Rose to use. The first Sunday, Ellie, Rose, and Jaquelyn played. But in the following weeks, they were joined by Deimos, Phobos, and Cupid. All but Jaquelyn and Rose played without gloves. It was easy for Ellie to play barehanded; she was used to catching balls at much higher speeds than anyone there was able to hit or throw.

This afternoon—the day before the picnic—Danny and Christina played, too, while Violet napped. Even though there was still a lot of preparation to be done for the picnic, they wanted to practice before the big family game. Christina couldn't catch or throw very well, but she surprised everyone with the bat. Danny was the opposite. He could reach anyone when he threw; however, even when Cupid, the slowest pitcher in the group, pitched to him, Danny either struck out or hit a short fly that usually fouled out. Jaquelyn, on the other hand, was talented in all aspects. Ellie thought it was too bad that she wasn't allowed to play at school or in a league.

Of the three brothers, Phobos had the best skills. He'd learned to play back in June, when he'd arranged the game with the celebrity players. As a god, he'd managed to pick up on skills quickly, and, even without his powers, his body seemed to remember what to do. He was easily Ellie's best competition.

Cupid and Deimos had never played softball before they'd begun joining Ellie on Sundays, and they needed a lot of practice to avoid making fools of themselves at the picnic. Ellie thoroughly enjoyed laughing at them, especially at Deimos, who was cute in every way imaginable.

Ellie and Deimos tried to be careful about the way they interacted together when they weren't protected by the helm, but neither were good actors, and, on more than one occasion, they were affectionate in front of the others. This happened more frequently while they were swimming and playing softball.

While the Garcias didn't seem to mind the flirting between them, Phobos and Cupid weren't at all subtle with their disapproval. Such unintentional displays of affection seemed to enflame the arrow of hate in Phobos's heart, which confused Ellie, because Phobos and Jaquelyn seemed to be getting along, and her parents seemed to be more accepting of it than they'd initially been.

That night, after they swam, turned out the horses, and ate a delicious bowl of stew, Ellie was shocked, when she returned to her room, to discover that the helm of invisibility was not where she had left it. She searched all the places it could be and came up with nothing.

The boys were stripping off their boots and clothes and getting ready for bed when she asked Deimos if she could have a private word with him outside.

In his stockinged feet and jeans, he followed her to the well. As upset as she was over the loss of the helm, seeing his strong, bare chest and abs in the moonlight lifted her mood.

"What's wrong?" he asked, when he sat on the stone ledge beside her.

"You know that thing we use—one of the most important objects in the world?"

His smile cracked his face in half. "Yes? It's also my favorite object in the world these days."

"It's gone."

His mouth fell open. "Seriously?"

"Do you think she took it back?"

"I suppose we couldn't keep it forever."

Ellie sighed. "It was good while it lasted."

She recalled the time she and Deimos had almost been caught in the stables by Phobos. Without them knowing, he'd followed them in there and had found her panties. She wondered if he knew about the helm. If so, could he have taken it?

Deimos sighed, too. "These next months are going to be unbearable now."

"One down, five to go."

"Let's pray they go by quickly."

"It won't be so bad, will it?" She wished she could say what she really wanted to say. She wanted to say that at least they'd get to see each other every day—even if they couldn't touch without drawing suspicion from the other gods.

"It could be worse, I guess."

After following Deimos and Ellie from the shack, Phobos snuck with bare feet across the pea gravel and back to his bed, where he removed the helm of invisibility. He hadn't felt this happy in weeks. Although he felt guilty for thwarting his brother's happiness, it lessened the rage throbbing in his heart to know that Ellie would not find pleasure in his brother's arms.

The next day, after their morning chores, Phobos joined Ellie and his brothers at the swimming spot to rinse off and relax. He was in a particularly good mood today and wasn't even bothered when Deimos, while pretending to be angry at her, dunked Ellie underwater. It was just an excuse to touch her—but, whatever. Phobos knew where the helm was, and they didn't.

As he dried off and dressed for the picnic, he could smell the chickens frying. He couldn't wait to sample all the good food brought by relatives from all over south Texas. Even more than the food, he was looking forward to the softball game, which would be fun whether he played with Ellie or against her. If they played on the same team, he'd enjoy sharing a victory with her—because no team could beat the two of them. If they played opposite one another, he'd enjoy competing with her, even if he lost.

Once he and his brothers were dressed, they helped Danny set up extra tables and chairs beneath the trees between the back porch and the well. Then they carried bags of sand, to use as bases, to the east pasture and created a softball field, making sure the bases were sixty feet apart. Ellie came out with a bowl of flour and used the flour to draw a batter's box at home plate and a pitcher's mound. She used what was left of the flour to make the bases more visible from a distance.

People began arriving after noon. Although Jaquelyn had a lot of pretty cousins her age and older, they gave most of their attention to Ellie. The boy cousins did the same. Most of the relatives brought softballs and t-shirts for Ellie to sign with permanent marker. They begged her to allow them to take photos with her, but Ellie declined. When

Phobos asked her why, she told him in private that she didn't want her coach, teammates, or mother to come across the photos on social media and wonder what she was doing in Texas.

After the last of the relatives had arrived, it was one o'clock and time to eat. The dishes had been set out in the kitchen along the u-shaped counterspace. Danny had everyone squeeze together in the house—there were forty-three in attendance, including one six-month-old baby—to hold hands in prayer. As was his custom, Phobos silently thanked Demeter and Hestia for their bountiful blessings, adding, as he always did, that he'd enjoy them much more on Mount Olympus.

Phobos sat with Ellie and his brothers at the table nearest the well. Phobos was surprised when Rose walked from the house, her paper plate precariously balanced in her little hand, to sit beside him. He would have thought she'd prefer to sit with her relatives. Lately, when they fist-bumped after she made a good joke, or after she hit the ball well during practice, she'd say, "Thanks, boyfriend." He hadn't thought much of it, but now he wondered if she'd developed a crush on him.

Ellie noticed it, too, and gave him a knowing smile. It thrilled him to be on the receiving end of her smile, and the arrow of love radiated in his heart.

The arrow of love had also won out on other Sunday afternoons, when he watched with admiration the sweet way Ellie coached Rose in softball. He knew Ellie had helped with kids' softball camps in the past, but, more than her helpful techniques, her kind and encouraging words and enthusiastic attitude had made Rose feel like a champ—and this made the love arrow in Phobos's heart sing.

Jaquelyn brought Phobos from his thoughts when she carried her plate to his table and scolded Rose. "You go and sit at the kids' table with Johnny and Theresa and them. This is *my* seat."

"I can sit here if I want to," Rose said without taking her eyes from her food.

Phobos tried very hard not to laugh. He didn't want to piss off Jaquelyn.

Jaquelyn was about to storm off, probably to complain to her mother, when Ellie said, "Just pull up another chair. We can make more room."

Jaquelyn smiled at Ellie. "Thanks."

Cupid jumped up and found an empty chair and brought it to the table for Jaquelyn. He put the chair between where he and Phobos were sitting.

"Thank you, Cupid," Jaquelyn said.

After everyone had eaten and the leftover food had been put away, those interested in being a team captain drew lots. Then a coin was tossed to see which team would get Ellie. From there, the captains took turns choosing their teammates from those who wanted to play. Phobos was thrilled when he and Ellie were chosen by the same captain. Danny and Rose were on their team, too.

As the teams huddled to come up with their positions and batting order, Danny whispered to Phobos, "If I hadn't ended up on your team, I would have separated you and Ellie. But, if Christina and Jaquelyn aren't going to object, then that's their problem, right?"

Phobos gave him a fist bump. "Right."

Because his team got Ellie, the other team was given the choice of playing in the field or batting at the top of the first inning. They chose to bat. Those who didn't have a glove were loaned one by the other team. There were enough to go around so that every fielder had one.

Ellie recommended to their captain that she play shortstop, Phobos play first, and Danny play centerfield. The captain wisely took her advice.

"What about me?" Rose asked.

"You should play right field, behind Phobos, to get anything he misses. Okay?"

"Okay!"

Phobos grinned as the arrow of love sang.

After spending some time warming up, Ellie then recommended a pitcher—Jaquelyn's cousin Oscar, who was around nineteen or twenty years of age. Ellie also helped with the batting order, placing herself fourth, after Oscar, Danny, and Phobos, hoping to stack the bases for a grand slam.

The other team didn't have a chance to score during the first inning. Ellie was a force to be reckoned with in the infield. She and Oscar didn't let a grounder get past them. Both threw a shot to Phobos in time to get a runner out. Danny got the third out when he caught a fly ball to centerfield.

When it was their turn to go to bat, Oscar made it to first base, guarded by Jaquelyn. Then Danny hit a pop fly that fouled near first, and Jaquelyn caught it. Phobos sent a grounder to centerfield and made it to first, while Oscar advanced to third. When Ellie hit a homerun, they all made it home safely. The entire team huddled together for high fives and fist bumps.

Phobos took the opportunity to pat Ellie on the ass as he said, "Nice play."

The smile she gave him in reply set him on fire.

The first inning was a huge success with five runs. Even Rose made it to first base, though Phobos was pretty sure that Jaquelyn let her.

When the game ended, seventeen runs to seven, with Ellie and Phobos's team the victors, those wanting to swim changed into their suits and headed to the swimming spot. Since it wasn't quite as pleasant with over thirty other people, Phobos took a short dip and then returned to the shack, where he dressed and put on the helm.

He amused himself beneath the helm by spying on others until the guests began to leave. He was about to return to his room to take it off, when he saw his mother surveying the homestead from the sky.

He'd forgotten that the helm afforded its wearer the ability to see gods invisible to the eyes of mortals. Even without his powers, he could see her. She was searching for someone or something. Was she searching for him? For the helm?

Before he could pray to her, Deimos appeared from the house, alone, walking toward the shack with a smile on his face. Aphrodite flew to the well and revealed herself to him.

"Mother? What are you doing here? Have you come to help us?" Deimos asked, his face full of surprise and excitement.

"You and your brothers have been an embarrassment to your father and me. Why should I help you?"

"Then why are you here?"

"Artemis knows about you and Ellie and about the helm. She reported everything to the entire council on Mount Olympus."

"Oh, no."

"She recommended that you be relocated and that the helm be confiscated. Everyone but Hades—who no doubt gave you the helm—agreed."

"No, Mother. Please don't do this."

"I have no choice. I offered to come as an effort to pull myself from disgrace. Where's the helm?"

"What do you mean? I don't have it. I thought Hecate took it back."

"So, she's the one who gave it to you?"

Deimos hung his head. "Yes."

"Do you swear on the River Styx that you don't know where it is?" Aphrodite asked.

"I swear."

"Then come with me."

She grabbed his hand, and the two of them vanished.

CHAPTER THIRTEEN

The Patient

After the last of the relatives had left the picnic, Ellie helped Danny and Cupid retrieve the sandbags from the east pasture before turning out the horses. Then she and Cupid returned to the shack to look for Phobos and Deimos, so they could head to the farmhouse together for supper.

They found Phobos sitting at the table with the lantern lit.

"Sit down. I have something to tell you."

"Where's Deimos?" Ellie asked, her stomach suddenly in knots.

"Sit down."

She and Cupid exchanged worried glances as they took a seat.

"I overheard our mother talking with Deimos not fifteen minutes ago," Phobos said to Cupid.

Cupid's jaw dropped open. "Aphrodite was *here*?"

"She said that Artemis had caught him and Ellie together and had told the council."

Ellie covered her face. "This can't be happening. We were so careful."

"Deimos was taken someplace else to finish out his sentence," Phobos said.

"Where?" Cupid asked.

"Our mother didn't say. They disappeared before I could stop her."

Ellie narrowed her eyes at Phobos. "Did you even *try*?"

Cupid squeezed her hand, but she pulled away. She'd been left with the two brothers she least trusted to protect her. One of them hated her, even if it wasn't by choice, and the other had once agreed to kill her.

And who knew when she'd see her sweet Deimos again?

She stood up from the table. "Tell the Garcias I'm too tired to eat. I'm going to bed."

"Ellie, wait," Phobos said.

But she ignored him.

She stripped down to her t-shirt and panties and climbed into bed. When she heard the brothers leave the shack, she allowed the tears to come. Hugging her pillow, she sobbed harder than she had in weeks. Poor Deimos, all by himself. It had been her fault. Ellie was the one who'd prayed for the helm. And having the helm had made her and Deimos comfortable expressing their love for one another—too comfortable.

When the bell rang before dawn the next day, Ellie didn't want to get out of bed. She'd been crying most of the night and, for the first time since arriving, had allowed herself to embrace the darkness.

Thoughts that she'd originally kept at bay by staying busy now swept in and took residence in her mind. What was the point? Why do anything? What would the gods do if she refused to get out of bed?

She didn't care. Nothing mattered. If the gods wanted to kill her, let them. If they wanted to torture her, let them. She'd come to realize that they'd never let her be happy, anyway. So why try?

"Aren't you coming to breakfast?" Cupid asked.

She didn't answer.

"Ellie?"

She turned over and faced the window.

"Let her be," Phobos said. "We'll tell the Garcias that she isn't feeling well today."

Sometime later, she was awakened by Phobos. He was kneeling on the floor beside her bed and pressing a hand to her forehead.

"No fever," he said. "That's good. I brought you some water."

He handed her the canteen. She took a few sips.

"What time is it?" she asked, noticing that it was getting dark outside.

"We just turned out the horses."

"Already?"

"Do you feel well enough to come to supper?"

She turned her back to him and hugged her pillow. "My stomach hurts. I'm going back to sleep."

"You have to eat something, Ellie. It'll make you feel better."

"Maybe tomorrow. Good night."

Ellie waited until she heard Phobos leave the shack before she allowed herself to cry again. She was worried about Deimos. Was he sad? Lonely? Frightened? She prayed to the gods to please have mercy on him as the tears sprang from her eyes.

Maybe he was better off without her. Everyone was better off without her. What purpose did she serve, other than to eat, to breathe, and to take up space? What was the point of her endless suffering and unhappiness? The gods of Mount Olympus would never like her, would never accept her. They would never allow her to be happy again.

And she couldn't go back to her softball team after she'd abandoned them. They all probably hated her. Her coach would want an explanation, and Ellie didn't have one. Ellie's scholarship was no good anymore, because Ellie had breached the contract by missing summer practice. What other coach would want a player who'd walked out on her team?

No, there was no life for Ellie to go back to.

And Phobos and Deimos were free of their arrows of love. They could go on to love other people. When their sentences were over, they could return to Mount Olympus with their powers, and go back to the way things were before. They could go back, but Ellie couldn't. She couldn't go back to her old life, and she couldn't move on to a new life with the gods.

There was only one thing for her to do: At the end of October, when her three months were up, she would not claim a purpose. Then, after she became mortal again, she'd kill herself, if the gods didn't beat her to it.

At least she had a plan. Now, she could go back to sleep.

"Is Ellie not feeling well again?" Christina asked the next morning, when Phobos and Cupid walked into the farmhouse for breakfast without her.

Phobos took his seat at the table. "No, but Cupid and I can work twice as hard."

Danny handed Phobos and Cupid mugs of coffee. "Does she need a doctor?"

"I don't think so," Cupid said. "But we'll keep an eye on her."

"It's too bad Deimos had to return home to help your mother," Danny said. "We could really use him this afternoon. It's time to round up and separate the herd. We need to sell the yearlings before the calving begins."

Jaquelyn brought Phobos and Cupid steaming plates of eggs and bacon. "I could stay home and help out today."

"You shouldn't miss school," her mother said. "It's your senior year. You need to graduate, in case you ever want to do something else with your life."

"But who will take care of the ranch when you're gone?" Jaquelyn carried her plate to the table and sat down to eat.

"I will," Rose said.

Everyone laughed.

Rose frowned. "What's so funny?"

"Nothing, *mija*," Christina said. "You will make a great rancher one day."

Phobos worked hard alongside his brother and Danny to get the morning chores done. Without Deimos and Ellie, it took quite a bit longer, leaving them less time to rest before lunch. After changing into their swim trunks, Phobos and Cupid looked in on Ellie. She was still in bed. Afraid to wake her, they went to the swimming spot to rinse off without saying anything to her.

At lunchtime, Phobos had an idea.

"Hey, Rose?"

"Yes, boyfriend?"

"Do you have an old toy or stuffed animal that you could loan to Ellie, to cheer her up until she feels better?"

"That's a good idea!"

Rose climbed from the bench and ran through the house toward her bedroom.

"You should take her a bowl of stew," Christina said. "I made it because it's her favorite."

"Thank you, Christina. I will."

Rose returned with a giant rabbit stuffed animal in her arms.

"Wow!" Cupid said. "That's a big doll."

"It's almost as big as you," Phobos said with a laugh.

Violet held out her arms for it. "That's *my* bunny!"

"Rosie-Ro," Christina scolded. "You can't loan Ellie one of *Vi's* toys."

Rose frowned. "But she never plays with it."

Phobos shook his head. "That's not cool, girlfriend."

Violet started crying until Rose said, "Fine," and handed the rabbit to her little sister.

Then Violet climbed from the bench and carried it toward the back door.

"Where are you going, Vi?" Danny asked.

"Ellie."

"That's cute," Cupid said. "She wants to loan her bunny to Ellie herself."

"I'll take her," Phobos said. "If that's okay?"

"Sure." Christina smiled and got up from the table. "But take a bowl of stew with you."

Rose crossed her arms and pouted. "I'm going to see Ellie, too."

"Of course, you are, girlfriend."

"Wait!" Rose said. "I forgot something!"

Rose ran through the house to her room and returned with a blue plastic case.

"What's that?" Cupid, who carried a glass of iced tea for Ellie, asked.

"My doctor's kit."

"Good thinking," Phobos said as he escorted them from the house.

When they reached Ellie's room, they found her awake and crying.

"Ellie!" Rose sat on her knees beside Ellie in the bed. "Are you better yet?"

Ellie wiped her eyes. "I don't know. What are you doing here? Hello, Violet."

Violet laid the big rabbit on the bed beside Ellie. "Foo Foo."

"That's what she calls the rabbit," Rose explained. "Bunny Foo Foo."

"Violet wants to loan it to you until you feel better," Phobos added.

Ellie picked up the rabbit and smiled at Violet. "How sweet! Thank you, Violet!"

"It was *my* idea," Rose added.

Phobos chuckled.

"Thank you, too, Rose," Ellie said.

"And Mimi made you some stew, because it's your favorite," Rose said. "Give it to her, boyfriend."

Phobos squatted beside the lower bunk and handed over the stew.

"Here's a glass of iced tea," Cupid said, handing it to her.

Ellie put the glass on the windowsill by her bed. "Thank you, everyone. I really appreciate it."

"You're welcome," Rose said. "Papa wants to know if you're going to help with the round up this afternoon, or if you're still too sick. You don't *look* sick—except your eyes are kind o' red. Are you going to ride Sherlock? He says Mo does most of the work, anyway."

Ellie sat up and took a bite of the stew. "Mmm. This is so good. I didn't realize how hungry I was."

Rose opened her doctor's kit. "Let me check your temperature."

Rose put her toy gadget near Ellie's ear. Then she took out her plastic stethoscope and listened to Ellie's heart while Ellie ate her stew.

"You're all better!" Rose exclaimed.

Ellie smiled at Phobos, which sent chills of pleasure down his spine.

"It's good to see you smile," he said.

"Okay, girls," Cupid said. "Let's get you back to the house, so Ellie can rest."

"Do we have to?" Rose asked.

"I think it's your naptime, anyway, isn't it?" Phobos asked.

"It's Vi's naptime, but I'm a big girl."

Violet crossed her arms, like Rose always did. "I'm a big girl, too."

"Then, come on, big girls," Cupid said with a laugh. "Time to get back to the house before Mimi comes looking for you."

Phobos was grateful to be left alone with Ellie as Cupid took the girls back. "How are you feeling?"

"Numb."

"Numb? What do you mean? Is it your blood circulation?" Phobos quickly massaged each of her legs.

"No, Phobos, no, stop. It's not that. I mean numb emotionally."

That hurt. He understood that she was heartbroken over Deimos's absence, but was Phobos not enough to make her feel anything? The arrow of hate threatened to overpower him as he gritted his teeth. He took a deep breath and tried to maintain control.

"Maybe some fresh air will help," he said. "Come to the round up. Give it a try."

Ellie laughed. "*Fresh air*? If I help round up the cattle, it'll be a dustbowl, don't you think?"

"Maybe some fresh *dust* will help," he said with a grin.

Her smile delighted him, overpowering the hate.

"Maybe so," she said. "I need to pee and brush my teeth."

He helped her climb from the bed and handed her the jeans that were still lying on the floor near her bed.

"I can dress myself," she said as she pulled them on.

"Fine."

"I'm sorry." She stepped into her boots and grabbed her toothbrush.

"It's okay. I'm just glad to see you up again."

He watched her leave the shack for the farmhouse with her empty bowl and cup. Even with her wild, unbrushed hair and red, swollen eyes, she was adorable to him.

Round Up

Ellie was in no mood to deal with Gypsy and was relieved when Danny told her to saddle up Sherlock instead. As they waited in the pen outside the main barn at the center fence, they watched Mo race out into the northwest pasture ahead of them to herd any strays back to the group. Then Danny, Phobos, Cupid, and Ellie followed on horseback to bring the herd in.

Like Ellie's mood, the clouds were gray. She wondered if they'd finally get some rain—not that it mattered to her one way or the other.

"Remember," Danny said, as they rode their horses uphill. "It's better to go slow with the cows. It'll take less time in the long run. If you try to move them too fast, they'll spook and scatter."

The cows were reluctant to leave the shade tree where they'd been congregating, but they were not willing to let the horses get too close. The cattle strode away from the horses, and it took careful coordination on the part of Ellie and the others to keep all forty-nine of the cows moving across the pasture in the direction of the pen. Mo was an expert at bringing any stragglers back into the fold.

To Ellie, herding the cattle was a lot like playing zone defense in basketball. She had an area to defend. She couldn't allow the cows to break her line of defense.

It took a full hour to drive the cattle from the most northwestern corner of the pasture down the hill across the thirty or so acres to the pen between the hay barn and the main barn. Once the gate was closed,

Danny told Cupid to block the gate to the main barn with Bailey while Danny opened it. Then Danny climbed back onto Chestnut and took Cupid's place.

With all forty-nine cattle in the pen at once, there wasn't much room for the animals to move. Ellie, Cupid, and Phobos kept their horses at halt along the perimeter.

"I'm only letting the yearlings through," Danny said. "Once the herd size shrinks, I'll need you to drive the cattle toward me—slowly. Remember, slow is key."

Then he added, "Cupid and Phobos, stay on either side and force any yearlings that dodge me back this way. I'm keeping three of the yearling heifers with the herd. I'll let you know which ones."

"Got it," Phobos said.

Ellie was amazed by how fast Danny got Chestnut to jump back and forth in a kind of dance to block cows while allowing yearlings into the main barn. But it took hours to separate them, because the smaller the herd in the pen became, the harder it was to guide them toward the barn.

It also became harder for Ellie as she used Sherlock to corral the cows, because she felt sorry for the frightened cattle. The yearlings were being separated from their mothers for the very first time, and they had no idea why. They were bawling and bellowing for their mothers. And the cows, too, were crying out for their calves and pacing nervously in the pen. It was heartbreaking to watch.

Ellie reminded herself that plenty of other animals left their mothers within the first year of birth—that she shouldn't apply human standards to the lives of other species. But a part of her couldn't help but think of the stories of slaves whose children were taken from them and sold to other plantations.

As the last of the yearlings were sorted into the main barn, leaving the cows yearning for their offspring, Ellie broke into tears.

"Ellie?" Phobos called from across the pen. "What's wrong?"

She wiped her eyes with the back of her hand. "I don't feel good."

Danny overheard and said, "We're pretty much done for the day. The boys can help me feed and water the yearlings, if you need to go lie down. Cupid, go ahead and turn out the cattle."

Ellie watched the childless cows being forced from the pen. They didn't want to leave their yearlings, which were in the adjacent barn and visible to them. They bawled and resisted, but Cupid used Bailey to corral them from the pen and into the northwest pasture.

The cows remained near the center fence and watched as Cupid and Phobos released the yearlings back into the pen. The yearlings cried out to the mothers, and their mothers replied. Even though the center fence still separated them, they seemed less nervous now that they could see and smell one another.

Then Ellie followed the boys on their horses to the stables to remove their tack. Ellie ignored the worried glances she received from Phobos and Cupid. How could she explain to them how she felt? How could she express her utter disillusionment—her realization that life—all life—was meaningless?

When Ellie refused to get out of bed that evening to turn out the horses or to eat supper, Phobos brought her a plate and a glass of iced tea, but she said she didn't want them.

"Is there anything I can do to help?" he asked.

"No. There's nothing *anyone* can do."

Not knowing what else to say, he left her alone.

The following morning, he brought her a biscuit and a mug of coffee, but she rolled over, putting her back to him, and ignored him.

After lunch, he brought her a sandwich and chips and was surprised when she accepted them.

"Thanks," she said.

"Feeling better?"

"Not really."

"Does anything hurt?"

"Nope. I'm just numb."

"Because you miss Deimos?" he dared to ask.

"Because of everything," she said. "Because nothing matters, Phobos. We eat, we shit, we deal with the shit of others, and we die, and there's nothing we can do to change it."

He furrowed his brows. Was she planning on reverting then? "*You* won't die."

"It's the only thing I *can* do. And I'm looking forward to it."

"I was under the impression that you'd changed your mind—that you were planning to claim a purpose and become a goddess."

She didn't reply.

Phobos brought a chair from the other room and sat there, watching her eat. She took no pleasure in her food. She had a glazed look on her face. What had happened to his Ellie?

He spent the afternoon helping Cupid clean the pen by the haybarn while Danny and his veterinarian worked with the yearlings to get them ready for sale. Then Phobos and Cupid rode out on Blondie and Bailey to check on the cows, who Danny said would be calving any day now.

When they were done for the day, they invited Ellie for a swim. Phobos was delighted when she agreed.

As they trekked to the west pasture in their swimsuits, Cupid said, "I'm glad you're finally feeling a little better, Ellie."

"I'm just bored," she said. "If I could sleep all day and night, I would, but I can't, and when I don't sleep, time crawls. So, I may as well force myself to do something to help pass the time."

"Do you think you should see a doctor?" Phobos asked, worried about her frame of mind.

"If it's not Dr. Kevorkian, it won't help me."

"Who's Dr. Kevorkian?" Phobos asked.

"It's too bad Professor Deimos isn't here to enlighten you," she snapped.

Rage surged through Phobos's heart. He grabbed her arm. "Now, just a minute, Ellie. I've been nothing but kind to you, despite how hard it is for me. There's no reason for you to be like that."

She yanked her arm free. "There's no reason for *anything*, Phobos."

He seethed with hate as they reached the swimming spot. He jumped into the deepest part, submerged, and tried to cool off—both his body and his heart. But when he resurfaced and watched her climb into the stream to soak herself, he felt the urge to crush her, to hurt her, to rail against her.

Cupid cut the tension in the air by doing silly tricks from the rope. When Ellie laughed, the hate stewing inside Phobos's very bones began to dissipate.

"Hey, guys!" Jaquelyn called from the east homestead fence as she slipped through the gate in her bathing suit. She jogged across the pasture with her cheerful disposition and perky young body, and said, "I'm so glad you're still here. You usually go in by the time I get home from school, and Dad says you'll leave tomorrow before I get home."

"Who's leaving?" Ellie asked from where she lay on a shallow rock near the bank.

"You. You're all leaving. You're taking the yearlings to the feedlot near El Paso."

"How far away is that?" Ellie asked.

"I'm not sure how many miles," Jaquelyn said as she climbed into the stream near Phobos, "but it takes about seven hours to drive there."

"Why do I have to go?" Ellie asked the boys.

"Don't you think a change of scenery will be good for you?" Cupid asked.

"I wish *I* could go," Jaquelyn said. "I begged my parents to let me skip school tomorrow, but they said no."

"Why do you want to go so badly?" Phobos asked her.

Jaquelyn's face turned pink, making Phobos feel like an idiot. She wanted to go so she could be with him.

He tried to save face by saying, "I thought maybe you wanted to go because the drive is scenic, or because there's something special about El Paso."

"It's a pretty drive," Jaquelyn said. "And it's fun to get to stay in a motel and eat fast food."

Ellie laughed. "I guess that would be fun for someone who eats home-cooked meals every day, but I'd take your mother's cooking over fast food any day."

"My parents *never* let me get Whataburger or McDonald's or Pizza Hut. Sometimes it's a treat to eat someplace else."

Phobos was happy when Ellie joined them in exercising the horses that evening after their swim. Jaquelyn and Christina joined them, too, while Danny watched the little girls at the main house.

Afterward, they removed the tack and headed to the farmhouse for supper, where a pan of lasagna was waiting for them.

"This is the best lasagna I've ever tasted!" Ellie said.

Phobos was pleased to see her appetite had returned.

"And this bread!" Ellie said. "Is it homemade?"

"Yes, it is," Christina said with a smile. "I'm glad you like it."

"Oh, my gods! It's *amazing!*"

Phobos and Cupid chuckled. Everyone seemed happier now that Ellie seemed more like herself again.

But it didn't take long for Phobos to realize that Ellie *wasn't* herself. After supper, after they'd returned to the shack and climbed into bed, Phobos was visited by Ellie. She came to him in her t-shirt and panties and climbed into his bed beside him.

"What are you doing?" he whispered—though he was sure Cupid couldn't help overhearing. "Not that I'm complaining," he quickly added.

"I know you hate me," she said. "You can't help it, so I don't blame you."

"I don't *always* hate you."

He tried to explain what he'd learn the night he'd been drunk at Night in Ol' Del Rio, but she interrupted him.

"Just listen to me Phobos," she said. "And I don't care who overhears this—Cupid, the other gods, whatever. All I care about right now is passing the time until November in whatever way I can. If I can sleep, I'll sleep. If I can eat yummy food, I'll eat it. I'll swim when it feels good. I'll work when I can. I'll do whatever. But, right now, I can't sleep, and I need help keeping the numbness away."

He propped himself on one elbow and looked down at her. "What are you saying?"

"Make me *feel* something, Phobos. Hurt me, love me—whatever you want. But make me *feel* something, so the numbness doesn't swallow me up again."

He couldn't believe what he'd heard. He stared down at her, wide-eyed, with his jaw dropped open. "Ellie, are you sure?"

She grabbed a fistful of his hair and tugged him toward her.

Both arrows ignited his heart. In a fit of rage and desire, he pressed his mouth hard against hers. He sucked on her bottom lip and pulled her onto him. She straddled him and took off her shirt, and he grabbed, kneaded, pinched, bit, and loved her.

Her moans of pleasure delighted him. He smiled up at her as he pushed her hair from her beautiful face, careful not to let her head hit the top bunk.

She shocked him by slapping his face. He threw her down on the bed beside him and mounted her. Anger surged through him as he pounded into her. She clawed at his back and bit his lip. She hurt him, and it felt so good.

<u>CHAPTER FIFTEEN</u>

Road Trip

Ellie awoke in the arms of Phobos. It was still dark outside. By the light of the moon, she could see his beautiful face as he slept. For once, his brows weren't knitted together in anger.

This wasn't going to work.

She'd meant to use him, to keep the numbness away, but realized now that she was incapable of having sex with him without feeling love, too. And she loved him. She'd never stopped.

Even though he hated her, Ellie's love for him reminded her that love was worth fighting for. She'd been overwhelmed by the darkness for the past few days in the wake of Deimos's disappearance, and she'd forgotten that there *was* a point, that there *was* a purpose. It was *love*.

And Deimos loved her as much as she loved him. She would wait for him.

She carefully disentangled herself from the arms of Phobos and crept back to her own bed. She hugged the giant rabbit stuffed animal and cried tears of happiness and relief. She didn't want to die. She wanted to live. And she wanted to love and to be loved.

She wasn't a lost cause, like the yearlings who could do nothing about their fate. She could choose to live and to make the best of whatever life offered.

She hadn't been in her bed long when the bell rang. Cupid jumped off the top bunk and gave her a knowing grin.

She flushed with embarrassment, because he must have heard her with Phobos last night.

"Good morning," he said.

"Good morning."

She pulled on her jeans and boots, grabbed her toothbrush and the rabbit, and headed toward the farmhouse.

Phobos caught up to her and Cupid during the walk over. He slipped his arm around her waist and kissed the top of her head, as though he didn't hate her. She wondered if he only did it to ensure more sex. She'd have to find a way to let him down easy, though she doubted that was possible.

"Good morning," she said. "Sleep well?"

"Best sleep in ages."

She wished it had been his *love* for her—rather than great sex—that had been the cause of his restful sleep; but she supposed it was better that he didn't love her. It would make it easier for her to choose Deimos.

They entered the farmhouse. The little girls were already seated at the table.

"Ellie!" Rose said. "Are you better now?"

"All better!" She handed the rabbit to Violet. "Thanks for letting me borrow this sweet bunny rabbit, girls."

Jaquelyn brought her a plate. "I'm glad you're feeling better, Ellie. You'll need your strength for the road trip."

"Thanks," Ellie said of both the plate and the sentiment.

Danny delivered mugs of hot coffee. "Ellie isn't going, Jackie Chan. Just the boys."

"Oh." Jaquelyn handed plates to Phobos and Cupid. "My bad."

Ellie sipped the hot coffee, feeling disappointed—though she supposed she didn't want to be a part of taking the yearlings away from their mothers, who continued to graze near the center fence, near their calves.

"Sorry, Ellie," Danny said. "I don't want to have to pay for two hotel rooms."

"That's okay," Ellie said.

"You wouldn't," Phobos said. "I think it would do Ellie good to come along. Cupid and I can sleep on the floor. She can have our bed."

Cupid didn't seem as willing to give up a bed, but, after Phobos shot him an angry look, Cupid said, "I agree. Ellie could use a change of scenery."

"If Ellie goes, I want to go," Rose said.

"Rosie-Ro, can you drive?" Christina teased. "Papa needs people to take turns driving with him."

"I can drive," the four-year-old insisted.

Everyone laughed.

"Do you *want* to go, Ellie?" Danny asked her.

Ellie shrugged. "I'm a good driver. But I don't want to be in the way." She didn't want to say what she was really thinking. What good would it do?

"You won't be in the way," Christina said. "Danny, take her along. I agree with the boys. It'll do her good."

"All right, then," Danny said. "Hurry and eat. We need to be on the road by nine."

"By *nine*?" Phobos asked.

"We should have started an hour ago," Cupid said.

"The horses can go a day without grooming," Christina explained. "You guys clean the pens and the stalls and spread the hay. The girls and I will handle the rest."

Danny set up a temporary chute in the barn to aid in driving the yearlings from the pen to the trailer. The mothers bellowed at the fence as their calves were, once again, taken from them. Ellie wished there was something she could do to stop the madness.

By the time they'd loaded the yearlings onto the trailer, it was already half past nine. They climbed into Danny's pickup and headed for El Paso.

They'd been on the road for a half hour when, Phobos, who sat in the backseat with Ellie while Cupid rode shotgun, shocked Ellie by stroking her thigh until his fingers brushed between her legs.

When she didn't return his flirtatious grin, he asked, "What's the matter, Ellie?"

If the radio hadn't been on, making it possible for Ellie and Phobos to speak quietly without being overheard, she wouldn't have replied. Since the music was loud, she said, "I can't."

His brows knitted together. "What do you mean, you can't?"

"I thought I could, but I can't. I'm still in love with you."

Quite unexpectedly, the smile that crossed his face was not angry or smug. It was gleeful. "I'm happy to hear you say that."

"You *are*? Why? So you can throw it in my face?"

Phobos frowned. "I tried to tell you the other night, but Deimos beat me to it."

"Tried to tell me what?"

"The beer—it numbed the arrows. For a short while, I was free of them."

"What do you mean by *them*? You can feel *both* arrows? Love *and* hate?"

He nodded. "It's been a constant struggle inside of me. But after the beer, I couldn't feel them, and that's when I knew."

"Knew what?"

"How I really feel about you—without the influence of the arrows."

"Oh." She bit her lip, still somewhat confused. "And how *do* you feel, without the arrows?"

"I'm in love with you, too."

Ellie thought her jaw would hit the floorboard if it fell open any further. She sucked in her lips, fighting tears. She was happy and worried at the same time. If Phobos *hadn't* loved her, Deimos would be the easy choice. But now—now what would she do?

"Ellie?" He searched her face. "I can't tell if you're happy or sad."

She laughed. "Neither can I."

"Why aren't you *happy*?"

"Because I'm in love with Deimos, too."

She could see the muscle near his jawline twitching. The expression on his face was proof of what he'd said about the struggle between the two arrows in his heart. More tears filled her eyes as she realized he was fighting to love her.

"I'm sorry," she said. "I know I should choose, but I can't. When I thought you didn't love me…"

"How could you think that? How could you give up on me so easily?"

"You hated me. Deimos didn't. I thought that meant…"

"That he loved you more."

She nodded. "And that you never did."

Phobos cocked his head to the side. "Listen, I don't know why we were affected differently, but I *did* love you and haven't stopped."

"Really?"

"The feelings have been there, bound up with the hate. It's hard to explain."

She glanced at the back of Danny's head before asking, "What about Jaquelyn?"

Phobos rolled his eyes. "A mistake. When Deimos beat me to the punch at the fairgrounds, I backed off. Even now, I feel like I'm stealing *his* girl. I don't want to do that to my brother. Jaquelyn was a distraction."

Ellie didn't know what to say.

Phobos squeezed her hand. "If you tell me now that you want Deimos, I'll respect your choice."

"I *do* want Deimos."

The muscle near Phobos's jaw twitched again. He released her hand. "Fine."

She brushed away her tears. "But I want *you*, too."

Phobos spent the next several hours during the ride to El Paso trying to process his conversation with Ellie, while she slept with her head on his shoulder. On the one hand, he was relieved to hear that she still loved him and wanted him. On the other hand, she was no closer to making a choice between him and Deimos than she'd been before they were pierced with the arrows of hate.

As Phobos had struggled with the two arrows over the past six weeks on the ranch, he'd believed that time and circumstances would reveal which of the two brothers was a better fit for Ellie. He believed their fates would become clearer.

But he was more confused than ever.

Because Danny was worried that they might not arrive to the feedlot in time to sell the yearlings before close of business—which would mean leaving the young cattle in the trailer overnight—he drove without stopping. If anyone got hungry, he had snacks, and if they had to piss, he had jars.

At one point during the drive, Danny turned off the radio and said, "I don't like to talk about this around the girls, but I want y'all to know this because I'm planning to sell off part of my acreage before Christmas. When I get back, I'm going to pitch the idea to Christina."

"Why would you do that?" Ellie asked.

"I'd rather lose half the ranch than all of it."

"Do you mind sharing why you're in danger of losing the ranch?" Cupid asked.

"We had to take out a loan against it a couple of years ago when my daughter Jessica got sick after delivering Violet. She went septic and had to stay in the hospital for months. We couldn't afford the medical bills, even with the loan. And I'm several months behind on the loan payment."

"I'm so sorry to hear that," Ellie said.

"Even today with the yearlings, we won't make enough to get caught up on the loan. I keep getting deeper and deeper into debt. My grandparents are rolling over in their graves, I'm sure."

"They can't blame you for trying to save your daughter," Phobos said.

"Of course, not," Ellie said.

"I'm not telling you this for sympathy. I just want you to be aware of what's coming. I'll sell off the uncleared land and the west pastures and go down to twenty head. I'll have to sell one or two of the horses, too."

"Isn't there another way?" Ellie asked. She knew Danny and his family loved their ranch and hated to see it cut in half.

"If you know of one, I'm all ears," he said.

"Can't the government help?" Ellie asked.

"I've taken advantage of every program I know of."

Phobos scratched his beard. "Why do you sell the yearlings to the feedlot instead of finishing them yourself?"

"I was wondering that, too," Cupid said. "The feedlots have to make a profit after buying the yearlings from you, so they must get at least twice as much per head once the cattle are finished, right?"

"Right. But it's cost prohibitive for me to finish the yearlings myself. The grain, the hormones, the vet bills—it all adds up."

"Do they *have* to eat grain? And are the hormones *necessary*?" Ellie asked. "Why can't the yearlings stay in the pasture and eat grass until they're ready? That sorting process seems so cruel to me."

"There's a growing demand for grass-fed, hormone-free beef and dairy products," Cupid added. "You should think about changing your business model before you sell off half the ranch."

"I appreciate your desire to help," Danny said. "And I've thought about converting to a feeder—I really have. But I can't change my business model to chase trends. People are into grass-fed and hormone-free beef today, but something new will come along, and the hipsters will rally around the new idea, and I'll be out of luck."

They arrived at the feedlot at three-thirty El Paso time. Ellie, who'd refused to piss in a jar, ran for the nearest restroom while the others waited in line in the pickup for their turn to be processed. When Ellie returned, she complained about how crowded the cattle were on the feedlot and how frightened the calves being processed seemed.

"Danny, how long will the yearlings have to remain here, in these conditions?" she asked.

"It depends on their weight, but, typically, about three months."

"They have to stay crammed in those pens with hardly anywhere to move for three whole months?" she repeated.

"Would you rather they go straight to slaughter?" he said with a laugh.

"There are worse things than death," Phobos said. "This could be one of them."

"It seems like there's got to be a better way for the cows *and* for us," Ellie said. "If you already know you're not going to be able to make your loan payments after you sell the yearlings, why not try finishing them on grass this year? What have you got to lose?"

Danny laughed again. "The *whole* ranch versus *half*, Ellie."

Ellie sat forward and leaned over the console between the front bucket seats, so she could look Danny in the eye. "If you sell the yearlings, you'll lose money for sure and miss the loan payments. If you finish them on grass, there's a *chance* you could come out ahead. I know this feels like a lost cause, but why not give it a shot before you decide to sell acreage and horses? Maybe you can save it *all?*"

Danny shook his head. "You want me to turn around without selling, after we just drove seven hours straight to get here?"

"Yes!" Ellie cried. "Do it! Please!"

"I'm afraid," Danny admitted.

Ellie glanced at Phobos. "Sometimes fear is what you need to drive you take the risks you might not otherwise take."

Phobos wanted to kiss her so badly for that. He winked at her.

She patted his thigh and sent chills of pleasure down his spine.

"If Deimos were here," Phobos began, "he would say that doing the same thing repeatedly while expecting a different outcome is the definition of insanity."

Ellie's brows flew up as she cracked a smile. "Way to go, Professor Phobos!"

He shook his head and chuckled. "Don't call me that, or I'll be forced to slap you."

"Phobos is right," Cupid said. "Um, not about the slapping. Danny, you've been doing things the same way and getting nowhere."

"Exactly," Ellie said. "Why not try something new? If finishing them on grass doesn't work, you can still sell the west acreage and get back on your feet. Can't you?"

"I suppose so."

"Come on, Danny!" Ellie cried. "Turn the truck around! Save the yearlings from suffering! Reunite them with their mothers for however long you can! And maybe you'll save your ranch in the process!"

Phobos was utterly shocked when Danny turned the truck around.

Ellie shouted, "Yay! Yay! You rock, Danny! You the KING!"

Danny shook his head. "Let's pray to God this works."

It was seven-thirty by the time they stopped at a pizza place and after eight when they arrived at the motel. Danny said he wanted everyone ready for the trip home by two a.m. That would give them five hours of sleep if they went straight to bed.

Danny turned on the television to a news station for white noise, saying he hoped it would drown out the sound of his snoring.

"I doubt anyone snores worse than Cupid," Phobos teased.

"I don't snore," Cupid insisted.

Phobos rolled his eyes and said to Danny, "He snores so loudly that I'm afraid one of these nights, he might die in his sleep."

"From sleep apnea?" Danny asked, as he kicked off his boots.

"From my hands strangling his throat," Phobos said with a laugh.

Ellie guffawed, which delighted Phobos.

Danny laughed, too, as he pulled the blanket and sheet from his bed. "You guys can use these to make a pallet on the floor. I don't need covers."

"Thanks," Cupid said.

"I don't think I can go to sleep this early," Ellie said. "I napped on the drive over. And I'm still too wound up about saving the yearlings."

Phobos had been thinking the same thing. "I'm not sleepy yet, either."

"Good. Then I'll take the bed." Cupid abandoned the pallet he'd made with Danny's blankets on the floor between the window and the bed and made himself comfortable in the bed meant for Ellie.

"Then why don't you two go gas up the truck?" Danny said, throwing his keys to Phobos. "It'll get us on the road faster. There's a station two blocks over." Danny pulled his wallet from his back pocket. "Use my debit card. Add some ice to the ice chest, while you're at it."

Ellie took the debit card while Phobos grabbed his bag.

"Why are you taking your bag?" Danny asked. "You're coming back, aren't you?"

Phobos grinned. "I don't trust my stuff around Cupid. He's always stealing my last pair of clean socks."

Cupid shot him a suspicious look but said nothing as Phobos followed Ellie from the motel room.

As they neared the pickup, Ellie asked, "Why are you *really* bringing your bag? I know that comment about Cupid stealing your socks was bologna."

"I'll show you." He leaned against the pickup and unzipped the bag to reveal the helm of invisibility. Then he quickly zipped it back up.

Ellie's jaw dropped open, but she didn't say anything. He wondered what she was thinking. She didn't seem upset. She walked over to the cattle trailer, which Danny had detached from the truck to park in a separate space before filling the water troughs.

"I'm so happy we're taking them back home," she said. "I wonder how the cows will react when their yearlings come back to them."

"I'm sure they'll be happy. You should be proud of yourself, you know. I thought it was a lost cause, but you surprised me, changing Danny's mind like that."

She beamed back at him. "Thanks. It was a team effort."

"I like being on the same team as you."

"We make a *good* team," she said with a smile.

He handed her the keys. "You better drive. I've only ever driven in London. I'm not used to the steering wheel being on the left side of the vehicle."

Ellie laughed and took the keys.

"I had a feeling about one of the most important objects in the world," she said, as she pulled away from the motel. "Just so you know."

He still couldn't tell if she was upset about him having the helm, so he didn't say anything.

The gas station was visible from the road, and it took less than a minute to drive there. While they were filling at the pump, an orange tabby walked up to Ellie and rubbed its back against her boots.

She scooped it into her arms and cried, "Deimos?"

"It can't be," Phobos said. "Can it?"

"He doesn't have a white mark on his foot," Ellie said without hiding her disappointment. "And his eyes are green, not blue."

"I wonder who he belongs to."

"He must be lost," she said. "I'll go ask the gas station attendant if the cat looks familiar to him."

Phobos waited by the truck to keep an eye on the pump while Ellie walked off with the cat.

When she returned, she said, "He said the cat's a stray and has been hanging around for a few weeks. Phobos, we can't leave him here to starve. Do you think Danny will let us take him home?"

"I doubt he'll want another mouth to feed. And I'm not sure how Julio and Iglesias will like it."

Seeing Ellie kiss and stroke the cat brought back happy memories.

"I can't leave him. I just can't. I won't let him be another lost cause."

"We may as well try to smuggle him home with us," he said with a grin.

After he bought a bag of ice and added it to the ice chest, Phobos found one of the sandwiches Danny had packed and fed some of it to the cat.

"He's starving," Ellie said. "He's probably thirsty, too."

"Here's a cup of melted ice from the chest." Phobos put the cup near the cat's mouth while Ellie held him.

The cat lapped up the water.

"What if Danny finds out and makes us get rid of the poor little guy?"

"We'll take him to a shelter. It would still be better than leaving him here."

Ellie flashed him a smile. "Good idea."

When they returned to the motel, they slept on the pallet on the floor between Cupid's bed and the window, with the cat curled up between them. Phobos didn't want to push his luck, but he couldn't help giving Ellie a kiss could night. He'd meant to give her a simple peck, but his lips seemed to have a mind of their own as they pressed hard against her. His teeth, too, seemed, of their own accord to bite, and his tongue penetrated her mouth and explored her neck without his permission. And once his mouth had gone that far, the rest of his body revolted, too.

As he made sweet love to Ellie, he prayed to Hypnos to keep Danny and Cupid soundly asleep.

<u>CHAPTER SIXTEEN</u>

A New Shack-Mate

Christina seemed shocked, at first, when they arrived home at nine o'clock on Saturday morning with the yearlings still in the trailer. Ellie, Cupid, and Phobos helped Danny to release them back to the northwest pasture with the herd after Danny explained his reasoning to his wife. Ellie felt awkward standing there on the dirt driveaway with the brothers as Danny and Christina discussed finances in front of them. In the end, Christina said she preferred what she called this "Hail Mary" effort over selling off the acreage, so Danny seemed happier with his decision.

With that settled, Ellie and the brothers got to work cleaning the stalls and pens, while Danny cleaned out the cattle trailer.

Although it hadn't been easy to smuggle the cat back to the ranch, once they got him there, Ellie and Phobos took turns using the helm to keep the cat out of sight of the members of the Garcia family. They were forced to let Cupid in on the secret, however, because there was no other way to explain the bowl of goat's milk Ellie kept on the floor by her bed.

They'd also managed to get Julio and Iglesias accustomed to the cat's presence by introducing them to each other at night, for five nights in a row, while the others were asleep, so the dogs would accept the cat as part of the family instead of seeing him as a predator.

Ellie called the cat *Deimos* when she was alone with him and *Kitty* when she was with Phobos, but Phobos must have overheard her when she thought she was alone, because he started calling him *Deimos*, too.

Deimos slept with Ellie at night and roamed the ranch during the day. During their morning chores, Danny was busy with the new calves, so he wasn't around to see Deimos following Ellie as she shoveled dung and spread hay. And when they sent Mo to bring in the horses for grooming, Deimos took off in the opposite direction. Ellie often saw him chasing butterflies in the west pasture.

They were at breakfast two weeks after they'd returned from El Paso when Danny said, "I noticed a stray cat roaming around the ranch. I'm surprised he hasn't been chased off by Julio or Iglesias."

"A cat!" Rose exclaimed. "Can we keep him? Please, Papa?"

"If the dogs don't chase him off, the coyotes will get him, for sure," Danny said. "You can't keep a cat, but, unless you're willing to kill it, you can't stop it from hanging around either. They aren't like other animals. They can't be penned in."

"If it bothers my chickens, I'll kill it myself," Christina said.

Ellie gave Phobos a worried glance.

In October, things changed. They moved the cattle from the northwest to the west pasture for the fall and winter. And because Danny was worried about the yearlings losing weight, they used Delores to drop haybales on the west pasture before dusk. The horses were kept in the stables overnight, groomed first thing in the morning, and then turned out so Ellie and the brothers could shovel dung and spread fresh hay in the stalls and pens. They brought the horses in at dusk, after dropping hay for the cattle. Dusk came earlier and earlier each day, making their work hours shorter. Suppertime was moved up to six o'clock.

The afternoons were spent felling trees from the uncleared acreage and chopping wood for winter. Ellie found wood-chopping to be harder on her muscles than any of the other jobs she'd had to perform so far.

But the cooler days made the work seem easier, and the shorter days gave them more free time in the evenings after supper to visit in the shack with the lantern on. One night, in mid-October, Phobos came to the table in the shack, where Ellie and Cupid had been sitting. Deimos was curled up in her lap. She and Cupid had been reminiscing about Ellie's time in his castle. Cupid had also told Ellie a few stories about Psyche. It was evident that he missed her very much.

They hadn't heard Phobos approach. He revealed himself from beneath the helm by placing a hand on each of their shoulders. Ellie was only startled for a moment, but Cupid had obviously had no idea that Phobos had been hiding the helm. The look on Cupid's face—wide eyes and mouth, lifted brows—conveyed just how shocked he was to see it on his brother's head.

Phobos took Ellie's hand and placed it on Cupid's, so that Phobos had only to touch Ellie for the three of them to be protected. Then, with his free hand, Phobos pulled a folded piece of paper and pen from his trouser pocket. Ellie quickly understood that Phobos wanted to tell them something that he didn't want to be seen or overheard by the gods.

Ellie stroked Deimos's fur and watched with curiosity as Phobos wrote:

I'm going to offer Artemis the helm in exchange for Ellie's freedom.

Ellie read his writing again, to make sure she'd read it correctly. Then she looked up at him, bewildered. Why would he do such a thing? This was his chance to be with her without Deimos interfering. Isn't that what Phobos wanted—a chance to help her to choose him over his brother?

She'd suspected that's what he'd been doing with the kindness he'd shown the cat: he'd been demonstrating what a good partner he would be if she were to choose him. He'd worked hard to fight against the impulse to hate her. He'd proven his love to her day in and day out.

So, why would he arrange for her to leave? Perhaps he was demonstrating how selfless he could be. Perhaps this was another attempt to win her from his brother.

She took the pen from his hand, but, before she could write her question, the door to the shack opened.

"Hello?" Jaquelyn called. "Ellie? Phobos? Cupid? I saw the light on and figured you were up. Anyone home?"

Jaquelyn couldn't see the three of them sitting around the table, because the helm rendered them invisible.

Ellie held her breath as Jaquelyn poked her head into each of the bedrooms and found them empty.

Then Deimos jumped from Ellie's lap and ran to Jaquelyn, where he rubbed his back against her leg.

"You must be the stray cat my dad was talking about," she said as she picked him up and held him in her arms. "Aren't you cute? What are you doing in here, all alone? Let's go look for the others."

Once Jaquelyn had left, Ellie quickly wrote: *Why?*

Phobos wrote in reply: *Because I can.*

Then he added: *I'd negotiate for all three of us, but I don't want to abandon Danny just when he needs us the most. Do you agree, Cupid?*

Cupid reluctantly nodded.

Ellie didn't know what to say. If this plan was an attempt by Phobos to win her heart, it was working.

The day after Phobos had revealed his plan to Cupid and Ellie, Jaquelyn pulled him aside after breakfast to reveal a plan of her own.

"I found the cat my dad was talking about," she whispered. "I'm going to talk my parents into letting me keep him. I'm going to use the rest of my birthday money to buy a litter box, so he can stay inside with us at night."

"Are you sure about this?" Phobos wondered how Ellie would feel about losing the cat to Jaquelyn.

"He slept with me in my bed last night," Jaquelyn said. "He and Mo got along fine. I don't see how my mom and dad can say no if I promise to take care of him."

"I hope it works out," he said.

As he was about to leave, to get started on the morning chores, Jaquelyn grabbed his arm.

"Hey," she said as her face turned pink. "I've missed spending time with you."

"It's been busy, with your dad tied up with the calves."

"Believe me, I know. If you weren't here, I'd be shoveling dung before school."

"I bet it's easier to make and keep friends when you don't smell like shit."

Jaquelyn laughed. "Definitely." Then she said, "Anyway, Oktoberfest is coming up. I really hope you can go. It's a lot like Night in Ol' Del Rio. There's a dance and carnival."

"Sounds fun," he said without making any promises. He didn't want to lead her on any more than he had already. "Have a good day at school."

"Thanks."

He followed Christina and the little girls out to the pig pen, where Laverne and the new Shirley were released for their morning walk in the east pasture. Cupid and Ellie were ahead of him, entering the stables. Danny had gone on Chestnut to the west pasture to see if any new calves had been born and to check on the weight of the yearlings.

When it was just the three of them alone in the stables, grooming the horses, Ellie asked, "Have either of you seen the cat? He didn't come home last night."

"He slept with Jaquelyn," Phobos said. Then he told her Jaquelyn's plan.

"I guess I'd have to give him up, eventually," she said. "Jaquelyn will take good care of him."

He noticed her eyes well up with tears.

Phobos said, "I'm going to do it today, before lunch."

Cupid and Ellie stopped brushing and looked up at him.

"Seriously?" Cupid asked. "Have you thought this all the way through?"

"I have."

"I don't know if it's a good idea," Ellie said. "What if things go wrong, and you lose your only bargaining chip?"

"I'll be careful," Phobos said. He wouldn't reveal the location of the helm until Artemis swore.

"I'd feel guilty," she added.

Cupid shook his head. "This never should have happened to you to begin with. Don't feel guilty."

As he finished up Blondie and started on Bailey, Phobos asked Ellie, "You haven't told me what you're going to do in two weeks. Have you figured out your purpose?"

"I haven't decided if I want one," she said.

Phobos felt his stomach cramp up and his throat get tight. "You mean, you might let yourself revert? Back to a mortal?"

"Maybe."

He didn't want to lose her. The arrow of hate raged alongside the arrow of love. He was pissed that she'd hurt him by allowing herself to remain a mortal and, one day, die. He wanted to say she was a selfish bitch, but instead, he asked, "Is it because you can't choose between me and Deimos?"

Tears fell from Ellie's eyes as she nodded.

After they turned out the horses and had begun to shovel dung, Phobos said, "Ellie, I don't want you to argue with me about this. I've made my decision, and it's final."

"What decision?"

"You'll say I'm being a martyr, but I promise I'm not. I'm doing this for purely selfish reasons, I promise."

"What are you trying to say, Phobos?" Cupid asked.

"I'm taking myself out of the running. I want Ellie to be with Deimos. I'd rather admire her from afar than watch her get old and die."

Ellie dropped her shovel. "I feel sick."

She ran from the stables to the outhouse. Phobos and Cupid watched her from the dirt drive, to be sure she was okay. When she'd finished throwing up, she left the outhouse and shouted, "Can you guys finish without me? I need to lie down for a minute."

"Go ahead," Cupid shouted back.

"Are you okay, Ellie?" Phobos asked, worried his words had caused her pain.

She shrugged and went inside the shack.

When the pens and stalls were clean and the new hay spread, Phobos and Cupid returned to the shack to check on Ellie. Deimos the cat lay curled on the bed with her. She was hugging the cat and weeping.

"This is all my fault," Cupid said.

Ellie glared at him. "Quit saying that. I'm glad I met your brothers and fell in love with them, even if it hurts. So, quit saying it was a mistake. It kills me every time you do!"

Cupid grabbed his swimming trunks and left.

Phobos knelt beside her bed.

"You smell like shit," she said.

"I know."

"I'm going to be sick." She jumped from the bed, startling the cat, who followed her from the shack.

Ellie threw up before she'd made it to the outhouse.

Phobos filled a plastic cup with water from the well, took a clean towel from the clothesline, and carried them over to Ellie, where she was bent over in the grass by the fence.

"Thanks." She wiped her face with the towel and took a sip of the water.

"Do you think you have a stomach bug?" he asked.

She shook her head. "I think I'm pregnant."

CHAPTER SEVENTEEN

A Spark of Inspiration

Ellie hadn't worried about protection when she'd had sex with Deimos because, honestly, she wanted to have his baby. At that time, she thought Phobos had never really loved her, and she was madly in love and excited about a future with Deimos.

Then, when Deimos disappeared, and she became numb and hopeless, she had only cared about making the time pass. She hadn't considered the consequences of her actions with Phobos, because she didn't care about anything anymore.

And the night in the motel with Phobos had been so spontaneous, that she hadn't thought about it then, either.

When she missed her period in the third week of September, she chalked it up to stress. Now that she was beginning to feel sick in the mornings and nauseous around dung, she was worried. If she didn't get her period next week, she would need to face reality.

Saying it out loud to Phobos just now took her a step in that direction.

She felt like the biggest hypocrite in the world for ever judging her sister for getting pregnant with Jonivan without a plan.

"Are you serious?" Phobos asked as he helped Ellie to the shack.

"I don't know for sure. I missed my period last month."

"Did you and Deimos…?"

She nodded.

"Oh."

She sat in one of the wooden chairs at the table. "So, there's no way of knowing who the father is. I don't think even a DNA test could tell us, since you and Deimos are identical twins."

He sat across from her. "Hera could."

Ellie lifted her brows. "Really? That's good, isn't it? I won't have to choose between you and Deimos, because the Fates will do it for me."

"I'd feel better knowing it was *your* choice," he said.

"We've been over this a million times. I can't. It kills me to even think about it."

"Why does it feel like my future happiness depends on the outcome of a crapshoot?"

"I thought you took yourself out of the running," she said, not attempting to hide the resentment and hurt she felt about his offer.

"I'm imagining myself as the father of your child. It's hard to walk away from that pretty picture."

"Then we'll leave it up to the Fates."

"That's such a copout, Ellie."

"Do you have a better idea?"

"Yes! Choose the brother that you can't live without. Haven't we been happy together these last weeks? Haven't you moved on?"

The truth was, she'd ached for Deimos every single day. Even though she knew he couldn't hear her, she'd found herself praying to him, almost constantly.

She knew, deep in her heart, that she would have felt the same way if Phobos had been the one to be taken away—she would have been praying to and longing for him. Looking at him now, she could see herself happy with him and their baby—if it was his baby. But as soon as she remembered Deimos, her heart hurt for him.

Maybe she would never be content. And if there were indeed a baby, she'd have to live with that.

"I don't know," she said.

He made her jump when he slammed his fist onto the table. "Fine. We'll leave it up to the Fates. But your condition makes me that much more determined to make the deal we spoke about."

"Let's wait and see if I miss my period. If I do, then I won't fight you. You can make your deal. I'll even promise to declare a purpose and become immortal, for the sake of the baby."

"What Baby?" Cupid asked at the door.

Ellie sighed.

"Ellie thinks she might be pregnant," Phobos said. "But she doesn't know whether the father is me or Deimos."

Ellie told Cupid about the deal she'd just made with Phobos.

"Do you know what your purpose is, then?" Cupid asked.

"Nope. Not yet. Any ideas?"

"You're the one who has to figure it out," Phobos said. "And you will. Just don't put off thinking about it. You only have two more weeks."

Great, Ellie thought. Pile on the pressure, why don't you? She kept her thoughts to herself, because she didn't want the gods to know just how clueless she was.

A week later, when Ellie didn't get her period, she and Phobos agreed to wait until after Oktoberfest to offer their deal to Artemis. Ellie had originally planned not to attend the dance and carnival, because she worried her presence in Texas would get back to her mother and coach, and she didn't want to have to answer any more questions from fans. But Jaquelyn convinced Ellie to wear a cowboy hat and to keep a low profile—no more carnival games that attract large crowds.

Ellie spent the days before the dance in a daze, unable to believe that she was going to be a mother—was already a mother. She was anxious to learn from Hera who the father was—anxious and terrified.

The night of the dance, Jaquelyn invited Ellie to her room to try on outfits.

Jaquelyn held a pink blouse up to herself as she gazed in her floor-length mirror. "If I tell you something, do you promise not to tell my parents?"

Ellie sat on Jaquelyn's bed, looking through the blouses Jaquelyn had set out for her. "I promise."

"I might not graduate this year."

"What? Why not?"

Jaquelyn plopped onto her beanbag. "I have a project due in English at the end of the month. We were told about it at the beginning of the year, but I kept putting it off. There's no way I can come up with something and finish it in four days. And it's thirty percent of our grade. I'd have to get hundreds on all my other assignments in that class just to pass."

"Oh, gosh, Jaquelyn! That sucks! What was the project supposed to be about?"

"Our teacher gave us three different epics to choose from. We were supposed to pick one and read it, write a book report about it, and create a poster illustrating the major characters and conflict. I don't have time to read an epic! My parents can't afford college for me anyway, so what's the point?"

"Could you maybe listen to the audiobook while you're doing other things? Or, is there a movie version? What were your choices?"

Jaquelyn looked up at her ceiling, as if the names of the works were written there. "Let's see, they were *Beowulf*, *Gilgamesh*, and *The Iliad*."

"Wait, *The Iliad*? Isn't that one about the Greek gods?"

"I think so. Why?"

Ellie jumped to her feet and grabbed Jaquelyn's hands, pulling her up from the beanbag. "Because Phobos and Cupid are experts on the Greek gods! They can help you get this project done—I'm sure of it!"

"Really? But, when? This project is due in *four days*."

"Let's skip Oktoberfest and work on it tonight."

"Skip Oktoberfest? Are you crazy? I've been looking forward to it for weeks! My parents aren't going. I was planning to drink and have fun—for once!"

"Would you rather have fun for one night, or graduate high school?"

Jaquelyn sighed. "You really think they can help me get it done?"

"Yes! And I'll help, too. My coach used to say that if you fall behind, run faster, and never give up. I know I haven't always followed that advice, but I try. I know you can do this, Jaquelyn. Come on. Let's go tell the boys."

Phobos was glad to get out of going to Oktoberfest. He hadn't been looking forward to the awkward problem of letting Jaquelyn down easy. So, after supper, he and Cupid told Ellie and Jaquelyn everything they knew about the Trojan War as they sat together at one of the tables in the farmhouse after supper.

Jaquelyn read passages from *The Iliad* aloud, and Phobos or Cupid explained what they meant.

Phobos cocked his head to the side. "It's too bad Deimos couldn't be here for this. It's right up his alley. He loves showing off what he knows."

Ellie smiled. "You miss your brother."

"So?" Phobos wondered why Ellie found it surprising.

Cupid clapped his brother on the back. "I don't think they've ever been separated for this long."

They hadn't been.

"I wonder what he's up to, and how he's doing," Phobos said. "I'm worried about him, if truth be told. I have you guys. He's all alone."

"I'm worried about him, too," Cupid said.

Jaquelyn furrowed her brows. "I thought he went home to help your mother."

"He did," Phobos quickly said. "But she sent him on a job all by himself. I don't even know where."

"Oh," Jaquelyn said.

"Let's get back to the project," Cupid said. "And to answer your question, Jaquelyn, Eris might have put things in motion with the apple for 'the fairest,' but my mother never should have promised Paris a woman that was married to another."

"Your *mother*?" Jaquelyn repeated with a laugh.

"I meant Aphrodite," Cupid said, as his cheeks turned red. "It's late. I must not be thinking clearly."

Jaquelyn turned to Ellie. "I told you this wasn't going to work."

"Yes, it will," Ellie insisted. "Let's get back to the story."

They spent three hours helping Jaquelyn understand the Trojan War and its major players. They discussed whether Helen was taken by Paris, or whether she left with him of her own free will. They talked about Hector and Menelaus and Agamemnon. And they argued about whether Agamemnon was right to sacrifice his daughter, and whether she'd been sacrificed at all. By the time they'd gotten through the major points of the story, Jaquelyn seemed confident that she could write a book report.

Ellie promised to help her make a poster when she returned home from church the following day, and she convinced Phobos and Cupid to help, too.

"You'd really spend your only free time helping me?" she asked them.

Phobos didn't think they had a choice. "Of course. See you then."

"Good night," Jaquelyn said.

As Phobos and Cupid walked with Ellie across the pea gravel to the shack, Phobos said to Ellie, "You really have knack for helping people out when all seems lost."

"It's too bad I can't help myself by choosing between you and Deimos," she said dryly. "Talk about a lost cause."

Then Ellie stopped walking. She stood there, under the moonlight, between the chicken coop and the well, as if she'd fallen asleep while standing up with her eyes open.

"Ellie?" Cupid asked.

"Is there a goddess of lost causes?" she asked.

Phobos glanced at Cupid. "Is there?"

"I mean someone who inspires people when all hope seems lost," Ellie said. "So, it would be different from a goddess of hope in general."

"I'm sure there isn't," Cupid said. "Ellie, does this mean…"

She jumped into the air three times before she said, "You're looking at the future goddess of lost causes."

Phobos smiled from ear to ear. He couldn't recall feeling happier. Whether he ended up with Ellie or not, whether he was the father of her child or not, he'd never have to watch her grow old and die. She'd be an immortal, like him, forever.

He took her in his arms and held her tight before kissing her forehead. "You're going to kick ass as a goddess, Ellie. Watch out, world, here she comes."

Ellie threw back her head and laughed. Phobos wanted to hold onto to this joyful moment for as long as possible.

CHAPTER EIGHTEEN

A New Deal

Sunday morning after breakfast, Danny, who'd been out on Chestnut, returned to the stables just as Ellie and the boys had finished grooming the other horses and were turning them out to pasture.

"You want to see something special?" he asked.

"If it's another cow paddy that looks like Jesus, I'm not interested," Phobos teased.

Danny laughed. "You know I was just joshing with you, don't you?"

"We thought so," Cupid said, "until you pointed out one you thought looked like his mother."

Danny laughed again. "Sometimes a rancher has to find entertainment wherever he can get it."

"It's a sad day when a person has to find it in dried shit," Phobos said, grinning.

"I want to see the special thing," Ellie said. "Where is it?"

"Just on the other side of the west homestead fence, behind the outhouse. I'll meet you there."

After Danny rode off on Chestnut, Ellie and the brothers walked across the pea gravel toward the haybarn and went through the gate to follow Danny. By the time they'd caught up with him, he'd dismounted and was kneeling on the grass beside a cow who was lying on her side.

"I thought y'all might like to see the miracle of birth," Danny said. "I saw the placenta drop a few minutes ago, so I knew she was close."

Ellie unconsciously clutched her abdomen.

Phobos gave her a reassuring smile.

Cupid knelt in the grass beside Danny and asked, "Are you going to help it along?"

"As soon as the forelegs appear, I will," Danny said.

Ellie went down on her knees beside the cow's head and gingerly stroked the mother. "There, there. It's almost over."

The mother lifted her head and licked her full udders before she lay back down again. Although she looked extremely uncomfortable, the cow didn't bellow like the ones who'd been separated from their yearlings.

The front legs emerged only to disappear again. A few moments later, they emerged again, and this time, Danny grabbed hold of them, so they wouldn't go back inside. The cow bore down, and a little snout appeared between the little forelegs. Danny pulled back with all his weight. Once the calf's head was all the way through, the rest of the calf slid out and onto the grass.

The mother got to her feet and began to lick the calf clean. The calf lifted its head and shook it, like a dog shaking water from its fur.

Ellie laughed. "It's so cute!"

"It's adorable," Phobos agreed.

"When will it take its first steps?" Cupid asked.

"Typically, within the first hour of birth. The mother will nudge him up when she's finished cleaning him."

"Thanks for letting us watch," Ellie said. "That was really something."

"Sure thing." Danny climbed back onto Chestnut. "Time to get back to work."

As Ellie and the boys left the west pasture, some of the other members of the herd approached the calf and its new mother. They watched as the mother cleaned her baby, but they kept a respectful distance.

Later, once the stalls and pens were clean and the new bedding spread, Ellie walked over to the outhouse and looked over the fence, searching in the pasture for the new mother and her newborn calf. She spotted them not far off, in the shade of a tree. The calf was on his feet drinking from his mother's udders.

Ellie clutched her belly again, anxious to meet her baby.

Ellie laughed at Phobos and Cupid while they sat at the farmhouse table together on Sunday afternoon, helping Jaquelyn with her poster for school.

"Poseidon has longer hair and a beard," Cupid said. "And his eyes aren't green. They have blue in them, like turquoise."

"*The Iliad* doesn't say that, does it?" Jaquelyn asked, as she pulled a blue coloring pencil from her box and pressed the lead to her drawing of Poseidon on the posterboard.

"No, but I have my sources," Cupid said. "And Hera's hair should be red."

"Like mine," Phobos said. "Ares's should be red, too. And Athena has black hair and gray eyes, that's why they call her gray-eyed Athena."

"Oh," Jaquelyn said. "Do you think my teacher will know?"

"If she's a good teacher, she will," Cupid said.

"At least she got Aphrodite right," Ellie said.

"Why did you make Zeus look so much older than the other gods?" Phobos asked.

"Isn't he the king of the Olympians?" Jaquelyn asked.

"Yes," Phobos said. "But he's the youngest of the six siblings. Demeter, Hestia, Hera, Hades, and Poseidon are older than Zeus."

"I don't think my teacher will care that much about that," Jaquelyn said, as she continued to color Athena's hair with the black pencil.

"Where's Hades?" Ellie asked.

"In the Underworld, the last time I checked," Phobos teased.

"Ha-ha," Ellie said. "I meant on the poster."

"He was neutral, wasn't he?" Jaquelyn asked. "I put the gods who helped the Achaeans on this side, and the gods who helped the Trojans on this side. So, I wasn't going to draw Hades."

"That's either stupid or brave," Phobos said. "I can't tell which."

Jaquelyn punched his arm. "Quit acting like these gods are real."

Ellie shared a smirk with the brothers behind Jaquelyn's back.

As happy as Ellie was feeling over having figured out her purpose, she had mixed feelings about the deal Phobos planned to make with Artemis after supper. On the one hand, she was excited to begin her journey as a goddess on Mount Olympus and to have a reprieve from the smell of dung. On the other hand, she would miss the Garcia family and the animals, especially Deimos the cat. Most of all, she would miss her beloved Phobos.

She'd been impressed with his ability to fight against the arrow of hate and to embrace the arrow of love. Some days, she'd forgotten about the arrows altogether. His love for her had become so obvious, that even Jaquelyn had seemed to abandon her efforts to win Phobos's heart.

Ellie's stomach did a flip-flop at the thought of living for three months without either brother. If she hadn't been completely happy with Deimos while Phobos hated her or with Phobos while Deimos was away, how would she feel without them *both*?

After a delicious supper of pork and bean soup with cornbread, Ellie walked with Phobos and Cupid across the pea gravel to the shack. They sat around the table, preparing themselves mentally and emotionally.

"I'll miss you so much," Ellie said to Phobos. Then she turned to Cupid. "I'll miss you, too."

"We're halfway there," Phobos said, as he turned on the lantern, which bathed the shack in light.

"How can you say that with such optimism?" Cupid asked him.

"I guess I'm a 'the glass is half full' kind of guy."

"We don't even know if this is going to work," Ellie reminded them.

"Ready to try?" Phobos asked.

Cupid and Ellie nodded.

"I'm going to make the offer silently, directly to her," he said.

Ellie understood that Phobos didn't want to be overheard by the other gods, who might want the helm for themselves.

He closed his eyes. Ellie flinched when the goddess appeared in the chair between the brothers.

"I want to see it," Artemis said.

"First swear," Phobos insisted. "You'll take her to Mount Olympus, where she can claim her purpose, and you'll petition Zeus and the court to pardon her."

"Are you sure you want to make such demands of me?" Artemis asked.

"I'm sure," Phobos said.

Artemis lifted her brows. "Then I swear. I'll deliver her to Mount Olympus."

"And petition to the gods to commute her sentence," Phobos quickly added.

"Fine."

"Swear it," Cupid said.

"I swear to petition the gods on her behalf, to have her pardoned."

Ellie couldn't believe Phobos's plan was working.

"Now, give it to me."

Phobos went to his room and returned moments later with the helm of invisibility. He handed it to Artemis.

Artemis smiled at the helm in her hands. Then she smiled at Phobos. "You might be interested to know that your brother Deimos has been restored to his godly status."

Ellie covered her mouth in shock.

Phobos's jaw dropped open. "He's back on Mount Olympus?"

"Not exactly," Artemis said. "Over the past six weeks, not long after your mother took him, he was condemned to return."

"Here?" Cupid asked. "We haven't seen him."

"No, you wouldn't have," Artemis replied smugly. "He was condemned to watch, invisible to mortal eyes, as the woman he cherished lay in the arms of his brother."

Ellie jumped to her feet. Mortification overwhelmed her as she recalled the many times that she and Phobos had been together. "How cruel! You cruel, cruel thing!"

"Watch your tongue, Ellie," Artemis snapped. "You have enemies on Mount Olympus who are ready to pounce on you the moment I deliver you to them."

"I do?" Ellie's legs began to tremble as she returned to her seat. "Why?"

"Have you forgotten about the reckoning?" the goddess asked. "I can assure you that the other gods have not."

Phobos reached across the table and took Ellie's hands. "Once my parents learn of your pregnancy, they'll protect you. Go to them as soon as possible."

"They already know," Artemis said. "We *all* know. Did you think we'd not monitor Ellie's every move, when she's been prophesied to bring our ruin?"

Phobos wished he'd never called on Artemis. Full of regret, he wished he could travel in time and have a complete do-over.

"Leave her here, with me," Phobos said. "Let her finish her sentence here."

"But you made me swear."

"I rescind my offer. Keep the helm. I won't hold you to your obligation."

"Only Zeus has the power to revoke an oath. The Maenads will hold me to it."

"There has to be something we can do," Cupid said.

"It's too late. Ellie is coming with me. And you boys will have to wait to learn her fate when you return in three months. Will she be swallowed by Zeus? Condemned to the Titan Pit? Or will she spend her days and nights in the arms of Deimos? Enjoy your agony, Phobos."

"Phobos!" Ellie cried.

Artemis and Ellie vanished before Phobos could object or say goodbye. He jumped to his feet and stormed from the shack.

Beneath the starry night, he shouted, at the top of his lungs, "FUCK!"

Cupid came up behind him and put a hand on Phobos's shoulder. "Deimos will do his best to protect her. Psyche will, too. I'm sure of it."

"What kind of chance do they stand against the other Olympians?"

"Hecate is on her side, I think. Hades may be, as well. Don't lose hope."

"If only I had the goddess of lost causes to pray to," he muttered dryly. "I could really use her right about now."

Since he couldn't pray to Ellie, he prayed to Deimos. *I'm sorry, brother. I'm sorry you had to watch us in silence. When you had her, you wore the helm and were invisible to me. I didn't have to see it. I can't believe they made you watch. I never meant to hurt you.* Then he added, *I hope and pray that you have her now, under your protection.*

Suddenly, Psyche appeared beside them beneath the moonlight.

Cupid gasped and threw his arms around her waist. "Finally! I've been praying for this moment for months!"

"I can't stay long," she said. "I only came to thank you for your faith in me and to let you know that you've restored my faith in you."

"Protect her, Psyche," Phobos said. "Please?"

"I'll do what I can."

"Stay, my darling Psyche. Visit me for a while."

"I wish I could. Listen to me carefully. You should know that the gods are divided. The majority on Mount Olympus believe that Ellie will bring our ruin. Zeus, Hera, and Ares lead that group. But there's a smaller faction of gods led by Hades who believe that the protection of Ellie will subvert the prophecy. It's no secret that I'm part of that group. I can't risk naming others to you now. Just know you aren't alone."

Psyche kissed her husband and disappeared.

"Wait!" Cupid cried.

But she was gone.

Phobos and Cupid stood beneath the moonlight, in silence. They were startled when the back porchlight on the farmhouse came on.

"Everything okay out here?" Danny asked.

Phobos wanted to say that no, everything was far from okay, but, instead, he waved, and said, "Sorry if I woke you. Everything's fine."

"Good night, then," Danny said.

"Good night," Phobos and Cupid called back.

They headed back to the shack in silence as Danny returned to the house and turned off the porchlight.

Cupid entered the shack and kicked off his boots. "At least we know she'll have other gods on her side."

Phobos punched his fist onto the table, nearly upsetting the lantern. "And I just gave our enemies one of the most powerful weapons in the world."

<u>CHAPTER NINETEEN</u>

The Abduction

Ellie closed her eyes to the blinding light of god travel as the pressure wrapped itself around her and Artemis. When she opened her eyes, she flinched and flailed, astonished to find herself flying over Florida on the end of Artemis's arm. Artemis held the helm on the end of the other.

"Where are we going?" Ellie asked.

"To Mount Olympus. Prepare yourself."

"You couldn't let me say goodbye? Why are you so cruel?"

"Bite your tongue!"

Ellie looked down at the Atlantic Ocean and had an idea. She would bite the goddess's hand and fall into the sea, where she'd have a better chance of surviving than with her enemies on Mount Olympus. As she was trying to get up the nerve, she worried the impact of her body hitting the water could harm the baby. Was the baby immortal, too, or could it die and never come back?

Then again, she doubted the goddess would let her go that easily. It would only piss her off.

She'd just decided not to risk it, when a spear whizzed by and stung her ear.

"What the hell was that?" Ellie cried.

"We're under attack."

Artemis put on the helm before she hurled an arrow through the air with her bare hand. Then, putting a finger to her lips, she sailed across the ocean and the continent of Africa toward the Mediterranean Sea.

Ellie came close to crying out for help many times along their journey, but she didn't want her baby harmed in the crossfire.

As they neared Greece, Ellie was confused when they flew past the mountains and dove down into a narrow gorge. They flew deeper and zigzagged this way and that, making Ellie nauseous. It was the chasm that Hecate had once taken her through to the Underworld. Why had they come here?

They arrived in the enormous foggy cavern where two rivers met. A tall iron gate, guarded by Cerberus, the three-headed dog, became visible as they flew deeper through the fog. They passed the old ferryman, who was boarding souls, along with a beautiful god with dark hair and bright blue eyes.

When Ellie and Artemis reached the gate, the huntress removed the helm.

Another goddess appeared beside them and took it. "Well done, Artemis. The 'attack' looked convincing."

"Your spear got a little too close, Persephone," Artemis said.

Ellie soon realized that the goddess beside them was the queen of the Underworld. Why had she thrown the spear?

"It went exactly where I wanted it to go," Persephone said, opening the gate. "Let's go inside, where we can talk."

Ellie closed her eyes to the blinding light of god travel, and, when she next opened them, she was standing before Hades and Persephone on the gold pavers of their throne room.

"I'm confused," Ellie muttered to Artemis. "I thought you were taking me to Mount Olympus."

"I will in two days," Artemis said, "so you can claim your purpose."

"Congratulations, by the way," Persephone added. "The goddess of lost causes—it's a fine purpose. And it's a pleasure to finally meet you in person, Ellie."

"Thank you," Ellie said, still confused. "Likewise."

"Yes, but now Artemis will need to request a pardon," Hades pointed out. "Returning Ellie to the ranch, stripped of her powers, was our only way of keeping her from becoming a prisoner on Mount Olympus."

"That needn't interfere with our plans," Artemis said. "I swore to speak on her behalf. I'm sure their spies already know this. I truly doubt they will agree to pardon her. Plus, it will give Persephone more time to rescue Hecate."

Ellie bit her lip. Was Artemis her friend or foe?

Artemis turned to Ellie. "It had to be convincing. I hope you understand."

As Ellie tried to piece together what Artemis was telling her, Deimos appeared.

Ellie covered her heart and gasped. "Deimos? Oh, Deimos! I'm so sorry!"

He flew to her side and wrapped his arms around her waist. "You have nothing to be sorry for, Ellie. I can't tell you how happy I am to hold you in my arms again."

Ellie felt the old feelings of panic he once caused in her while they were at Cupid's castle.

"Why don't you take her to her guest chambers, Deimos," Hades said. "You can brief her on our plans."

"Yes, Lord Hades," Deimos said. "Thank you."

Deimos led Ellie from the throne room, down a winding hall, and through a thick wooden door.

"When we figured out that Phobos was planning to trade the helm for your freedom, Hades came up with a plan to bring you here," Deimos explained.

The room was oval-shaped, and, like other rooms in the palace, sparkled from the light of the river of fire reflecting on precious stones embedded in the walls. A stalagmite on one end of the room held a flat piece of granite that served as a tabletop between two wooden chairs. On the other end of the room was a large bed with fluffy pillows and a thick, white comforter. Stalactites hung over the bed like icicles shimmering in a winter wonderland. Not far from the bed, running water dripped into a basin, the size of a bath.

"It's beautiful!" Ellie cried. "I've never seen such a fantastical place."

"It's not Mount Olympus, but it will do."

"Poor Phobos." Ellie plopped onto the foot of the bed. "Artemis left him in agony. Is there any way to get a message to him, to let him know I'm okay?"

"Now that we have the helm, yes. But it will have to wait until we rescue Hecate. We can't risk losing it before then. And, if all goes according to plan, you'll be back on the ranch before too long, anyway."

"What? Why?"

"We don't expect Zeus to pardon you. In fact, we don't want him to."

"I don't understand. Why not?"

"Commuting your sentence won't change the fact that he and his followers believe you'll be the cause of their downfall. If you aren't powerless on the ranch, they'll want to confine you in some other way—imprison you, swallow you."

"Oh, fuck."

"I don't mean to frighten you, but it's better that you return to the ranch," his voice cracked as he added, "and continue on with Phobos."

"Oh, Deimos! I'm mortified. If I'd known that you were there…"

He sat on the bed beside her. "Stop. It's okay. I heard your prayers and understood what was in your heart. I've come to terms with the fact that you love us both."

"You *have?*"

He put his hand on her belly. "Maybe it's because I believe the child *must* be mine. All those nights beneath the helm…"

Ellie smiled as she remembered the fun they'd have. "I'm so happy to see you again."

He squeezed her hand. "I'm so happy to *touch* you again. And I'm so proud of you! The goddess of lost causes! Phobos was right when he said you're going to be a kick-ass goddess."

"I'd forgotten the affect you have on me—the panic. I'm going to have to get used to it again."

"Only until you get your powers back."

"Tell me what's going on. Is Artemis really on my side? Why would she say such terrible things to Phobos? And when did Hecate get captured?"

"I promise to explain everything to you, Ellie, but wouldn't you like to get cleaned up?"

"I smell bad, don't I? I never really felt like I could ever get away from the stench of manure on the ranch."

Deimos laughed. "I felt the same way."

"A bath and a clean change of clothes sounds heavenly."

"That water in the pool is warm, unlike the water on the ranch. And you're allowed to use soap."

"Imagine that!"

Suddenly feeling modest—because she hadn't seen him in six weeks—she quickly stepped out of her boots and clothes and climbed into the warm water. The basin was deeper and longer than a standard bathtub, and she sighed with pleasure as she stretched her legs and leaned her head back on the ledge. She submerged to rinse her face and hair. It was soothing and refreshing at the same time. When she came up again and blinked the water from her eyes, she was overcome by panic until she saw that Deimos had climbed in beside her.

"Do you mind?" he asked.

Her smile reached her ears. She took a deep breath and fought the urge to flight or flee. "Not one bit."

Monday morning at breakfast, Phobos entered the farmhouse with Cupid and said, "I have some bad news."

Rose looked up at him from where she sat at the table beside Violet. "What's wrong, boyfriend?"

"Phobos?" Christina came from the kitchen, wiping her hands on her apron. "You look terrible. What's happened?"

He rubbed his eyes, swollen from the hours of tears he'd shed in misery and anger throughout the night as he'd pleaded with his parents, and any god who'd listen, to help Ellie.

Cupid put a hand on Phobos's shoulder and said, "Artemis came by last night. Ellie had a family emergency and needed to return home immediately."

"Oh, no!" Jaquelyn cried.

"Did she say what the emergency was?" Danny asked.

Phobos shook his head. "That's the agonizing part. She left without giving us any assurances that Ellie and her family would be okay."

"I'm so sorry to hear that!" Jaquelyn said.

"Why didn't you say something last night?" Danny asked. "That's why you shouted in frustration, isn't it?"

"I thought it best to wait and tell you today, so the news wouldn't interfere with your sleep."

"Phobos and I didn't sleep a wink," Cupid said.

"Is there anything we can do?" Christina asked.

Phobos fought tears. He'd never seen the goodness in humanity as he'd seen it here, with the Garcia family. He regretted the many times he put himself before their needs—centuries of selfishness. These people—all people—deserved better from the gods.

"Pray," he said. "Pray for their safety."

"You bet," Danny said. "And if you boys need some time…"

Cupid shook his head. "No. We'll be fine. We won't let you down."

"You worry about the calves," Phobos added. "We'll take care of everything else."

"You boys are a godsend," Christina said as she gave Phobos and Cupid a hug.

Phobos sat at the table across from the girls—he'd been joining them at the family table ever since Deimos's disappearance—and sipped the hot coffee.

Cupid sat beside him as Jaquelyn put plates of steaming food in front of them.

"Thank you," Cupid said to Jaquelyn.

"Is Ellie going to be okay?" Rose asked Phobos.

"I hope so, girlfriend. I really do."

Later that day, about an hour before dusk, after the last of the firewood from a tree they'd recently felled had been chopped and stacked, Christina called Phobos and Cupid over to the back porch, where she asked them to join her and the girls for some fishing.

"We're going to catch tonight's supper." Christina turned to her granddaughters. "Isn't that right, *mis hijas*?"

The two little girls nodded. They each carried an empty plastic container that once held sour cream in it.

Rose took Phobos by the hand and pulled him around to the front of the homestead.

"Where are we going?" he asked her with a laugh.

"You'll see."

They walked down the drive, past the compost bin and garage, toward the family garden.

"Wait for me!" Violet shouted as she ran to catch up.

Phobos turned back to see Cupid helping Christina with the rods, reels, and tackle box.

"Lookie here." Rose pointed to the ground. "This is where we catch the bait."

She knelt in the dirt and used her bare hands to dig around.

"That's a big one!" she said, as a worm tried to scramble away.

She caught it on one end and dropped it into her empty sour cream container.

Violet soon joined her on the dirt but had less luck catching anything. Phobos knelt in the dirt beside her to help.

A memory of Hermes teaching Phobos and Deimos to fish when they were very small made him grin. They'd snuck away from their parents without telling them where they were going, and they'd camped for days at a place Hermes knew. When they'd returned to Mount Olympus, they'd discovered that Aphrodite, who'd been overwhelmed by fear and panic, had forced every deity she knew to go looking for them. She insisted that they abandon their efforts in the Trojan War until her boys were found. When she'd learned that her sons had put her through her misery of their own volition and hadn't been abducted by a monster or some other enemy, she'd named them Fear and Panic—Phobos and Deimos—and that's how they got their names and their duties.

Once they were given their names and duties, he and his brother were sent to the battlefields to bring fear and panic to the Achaean warriors.

His parents had been using them ever since.

To ensure they would be strong, tough, and heartless, his father used to make Phobos and Deimos fight one another with swords or spears to the death. At first, Phobos hated being forced to hurt his brother, and he'd tremble and cringe and cry. But as the fights became part of their routine, Phobos relished his victories and looked forward to avenging himself after losses.

But there was no one he loved as much as he loved his brother—except for Ellie.

He thought of the baby growing inside of Ellie's womb and hoped it was his. If the babe did belong to him—hell, even if it didn't—he'd love it and care for it and make sure it *knew* it was loved. He'd never make the child a weapon like his parents had made him and his brother.

Now, he prayed to his brother and to Psyche and to Hades: *Please keep Ellie and the baby safe. I beg of you to do what you can to keep them from the hands of our enemies.*

CHAPTER TWENTY

The Underworld

Ellie closed her eyes as she lay beside Deimos in the white bed beneath the shimmering stalactites in the guest chamber of the Underworld palace. Deimos softly stroked her arm and told her to get some rest. But too many questions plagued her. She knew she wouldn't sleep soundly until she had them answered. And the panicky feeling he incited in her wasn't helping.

"Artemis hates me. When did she become my ally?" Ellie asked.

Deimos propped himself on an elbow and smiled down at her. "Over time, she came to see you as I see you. You won her heart in the way you cared for the Garcias and their animals."

"Really?"

"You should have seen how pleased she was when you convinced Danny to leave the feedlot with the yearlings on the trailer."

"But she's a huntress. Why did that please her?"

"It was right up her alley," he said. "She advocates for the responsible treatment of animals, especially those we consume."

"I didn't know that."

"She's more exacting with her punishment on irresponsible hunters and ranchers than on anyone else."

"Oh. Good for her."

"Why do I get the feeling that you still don't like her?"

Ellie pulled the thick comforter closer to her neck and sighed. "Whose idea was it to force you to watch? That was heartless and cruel."

"Mine."

Ellie sat up. "Deimos, why? Why would you put yourself through that?"

He pulled her back down in the bed beside him and wrapped an arm around her shoulders. "I begged my mom not to let me be taken to some other ranch. I begged her to find a way to keep me there with you, so I could watch over you."

"But—"

"Aphrodite didn't think Zeus and the other gods would agree to it. She said they wanted to teach me a lesson, to keep me in my place."

"I don't understand. I thought they'd sent us there to punish Cupid. You and Phobos and I, we didn't deserve it. We didn't do anything wrong. The only thing we were guilty of was loving one another."

"Phobos and I took off with you, remember? We wanted to protect you from Zeus and my father."

"But you couldn't help it. The arrow of love…"

"I'm sure we would have done it even without the arrow."

"You can't know that."

He played with her curly hair, still damp from her bath. "There's an understood hierarchy among the deities. Zeus has the most power and is king. His brothers Hades and Poseidon are second to him in rank."

"What about their wives?"

"It's still a fairly patriarchal system. Hera is just as gifted as Poseidon and Hades but not given near the respect."

"That sucks."

"The gods have been slower to evolve than humanity."

"Sure sounds like it."

"Demeter and Hestia also have tremendous power, but they rarely assert it."

"I wonder why?"

"They remain loyal to Zeus and defer to his judgment."

"Hmm. I'll never be like that, just so you know."

He playfully kissed the tip of her nose. "Good. I wouldn't want you to be."

"You still haven't explained why the other gods wanted you to suffer so much." Ellie thought to herself that this is where Phobos would say, "Get to the point, Professor Deimos."

"Anyway, the children of Zeus are the next in rank—that includes my mother and father. And their children are considered the lesser gods. Hecate, and other Titans who defected during the Titan War, are also treated as lesser gods, even though their powers are often equal to that of Poseidon and Hades."

"Wow. I didn't know that."

"So, when Hecate brought us the helm, Artemis saw it as a subversion of the council's authority and reported it."

"I take it I hadn't yet won her over."

"She was struggling and conflicted. Zeus is her father, you know."

"Don't make excuses for her. It was a dick move to tell on us."

Deimos laughed. "Well, Hecate was captured shortly after, for colluding with the prisoners. Artemis was tasked with finding the helm, but we continued to elude her. It was during that time, that she changed sides."

"I guess if there's a bitch in the house, it's better to have her with you than against you."

"She can definitely be a bitch sometimes, as she was when I was first condemned to watch."

"How did you get the gods to give you back your powers?"

"It was the only way I could watch you without being seen by you. My mother convinced the council that I'd suffer more by watching you and Phobos as a god than by shoveling dung as a man."

"Does your mother know that you're helping me?"

"She thinks I'm under Artemis's supervision."

"But you have your *powers*. Weren't they afraid you'd intervene?"

Deimos smiled wide. "I *did* intervene, whenever I could, without drawing suspicion."

"What? How? What did you do?"

"I'm not proud of *everything* I did, but there's one thing I'm proud of."

"Tell me."

"While you and my brothers were trying to talk Danny into turning the truck around at the feedlot, I touched Danny's heart with a tiny bit of panic, hoping he would flee."

"So, you deserve the credit. Not me."

"Not true. My touch only worked because you brought him to the edge."

"Hmm."

"Like you said to Phobos, it was a team effort."

Ellie blushed. She didn't like being reminded that Deimos had heard and seen *everything*.

"Now tell me something you did that you *aren't* proud of," Ellie said with a smile.

Now it was his turn to blush. "Okay, let's see."

"Deimos! Out with it!"

"I would lie close to you at night, even when you were with Phobos."

"Seriously?"

"I was careful not to touch you. I couldn't risk it. But once, I scared the hell out of the cat you called Deimos." He kissed her. "That was cute, by the way. It made me so happy."

"What else did you do?"

Deimos laughed. "Well, I'm not sure I want to confess *everything*."

She punched his chest. "Come on, Deimos! Fess up!"

"I will tell you *one more* thing."

"Okay. I'm listening."

"Remember that morning when you and Phobos were grooming the horses while Cupid had gone to help Danny with a newborn? The time you'd taken a break to make out?"

Ellie blushed. Then she recalled what had happened. Sherlock had urinated on the back of Phobos's jeans.

"I may have coaxed Sherlock into relieving his bladder at that particular moment."

"Deimos!"

The two of them laughed and laughed. It felt good to laugh, with so much scary shit going on.

Once they'd settled down in each other's arms again, Deimos said, "I need to tell you the plan we've come up with to rescue Hecate while Artemis takes you to claim your purpose."

She took a deep breath. As much as she wished she could giggle and pretend that everything was okay, she knew that it wasn't. While she lay in a silky cream nightgown in Deimos's arms laughing, Phobos was worried about what had become of her.

She hated that she couldn't get a message to him right away.

And there were gods that believed she was their downfall. They wanted to kill her or imprison her.

"Tell me."

"Tomorrow, when Artemis takes you to Mount Olympus…"

She sat up. "*Tomorrow*? I thought I had *two days*?"

"Artemis was still operating on Central Standard Time when she said that. We're eight hours ahead over here, and we lost another hour yesterday when the clocks leapt ahead from daylight savings time to standard time."

"How much time do I have, then?"

"I'd say about twenty hours—give or take an hour."

"Oh, gods. I'm scared."

"It's a solid plan. Hear me out. Okay?"

Ellie took another deep breath and nodded as she slowly exhaled.

Deimos sat up in the bed, too, and squared himself to her. "The loyalists—that's what those loyal to Zeus call themselves—don't suspect that Artemis has defected."

"I had that much figured out."

"Tomorrow, she's going to take you to Mount Olympus and claim that the two of you were captured by the rebels—that's what the loyalists are calling us. She'll say she just escaped but not without losing the helm."

"You think they're going to believe her?"

"We hope so. And, while she's making her speech, Persephone and Hypnos will be there, beneath the helm, trying to free Hecate."

"Where is Hecate being held?"

"In Demeter's rooms. Demeter is away, at her winter cabin on Mount Kronos."

"Won't they expect someone to use the helm to free Hecate, once they learn it was taken from Artemis?"

"Yes, but the hope is that they won't have learned it in time to do anything about it."

"It sounds too easy."

"It won't be. Hecate is heavily guarded by Iris and Nike and two of Aphrodite's Charities. And because Hecate has a way with spells and other forms of witchcraft, Zeus paralyzed her with his lightning bolt."

"That's terrible! Will Hecate ever recover?"

"Nobody knows. We can only hope."

Tears sprang to Ellie's eye. "I'm the one who prayed for the helm. She's paralyzed because of me."

"I prayed for it, too. We can't blame ourselves. We didn't paralyze her. Zeus did."

"Persephone and Hypnos will have to carry her out without the guards noticing."

"Hypnos will attempt to put the guards into the deep boon of sleep. It doesn't always work on gods, but if it does, it'll make their mission so much easier."

"And if it doesn't?"

"Hypnos will create a diversion to distract the guards. Either way, they'll soon know that Hypnos is on our side."

Ellie sucked in her lips. It seemed like such a lost cause. Then she sat up. "When will I claim my purpose? And how will I protect myself once I do?"

"Artemis will cue you. When she's finished revealing how you two were abducted and what she learned from the rebels, she'll announce that you're ready to claim your purpose. She'll also keep her oath to Phobos and petition that your sentence to serve on the ranch for six months be commuted to three, but she'll admit that her obligation to petition them was coerced in exchange for the helm."

"What if the loyalists decide to pardon me anyway?"

Deimos glanced at her abdomen.

She clutched it. "What? What are you not saying?"

CHAPTER TWENTY-ONE

Plans

Is this the fish I caught, Mimi?" Rose asked at the supper table, where she sat beside her sister and across from Phobos and Cupid.

Christina finished serving the plates and sat between her granddaughters. "I think that one *is* yours, *mija!*"

Danny led them in prayer, and, because Phobos didn't know if Demeter and Hestia were on his side, he used the time to plead to Psyche, Hades, and Deimos to protect Ellie and her baby.

"I'm surprised Artemis hasn't called or dropped by with news about Ellie and her family," Danny said, when he'd finished his prayer.

"I think it's part of our punishment," Phobos said before taking a sip of his iced tea.

"That's horrible," Jaquelyn said. "I hope you're kidding."

"He's not," Cupid said. "Our family can be cruel."

"I'm beginning to feel bad for agreeing to Artemis's terms," Danny said. "I agreed, because I thought you were parolees. When you told me you weren't, I thought that it was a family affair and none of my business. But now, I'm worried you've been wrongly punished and that I should have been paying you more than room and board for your hard work."

"I'd hardly call that shack proper *room*," Christina added.

Phobos shook his head. "We don't want money."

"We don't need it, either," Cupid insisted. "And I haven't minded the work. It's been rewarding—especially working with the horses and the newborns."

"It's had its moments," Phobos said with a grin. "I can't say I wouldn't rather be doing something else, though, to be honest."

Christina and Danny laughed.

"The rancher's life isn't for everyone," Christina said.

"Amen," Phobos said.

"The hardest part for me has been missing my wife," Cupid said.

"I didn't realize you were married," Jaquelyn said.

"Oh, yes. For a very long time. It's been a hard adjustment, living so many months without her."

"You can't have been married for a *very* long time," Danny said with a laugh. "That doesn't happen until you get to be my age."

"Maybe it just *seems* like a very long time," Phobos teased.

"Do you have any children?" Christina asked Cupid.

"Not yet." Cupid glanced at Phobos.

Jaquelyn noticed. "What about you, Phobos? You're not married, but do *you* have any children?"

"None that I know of," he said with a laugh, but he found himself laughing alone.

Fortunately for Phobos, Rose changed the subject by asking what he was going to be for Halloween.

"A ranch hand," Phobos said.

He was glad when that joke *did* get him a few laughs.

"You want to know what I'm going to be?" Rose asked.

"Let me guess," Phobos said. "A witch?"

"No."

"A ghost?"

Rose shook her head.

"A fairy?"

"No. Do you want me to tell you? Or do you want to keep guessing?"

"Maybe you should tell him," Cupid said.

"I'm going to be a zombie!" she said. "Mimi is going to put fake blood on me, aren't you, Mimi? I'll look like I'm dead, but I won't be!"

"You'll be the living dead," Jaquelyn said in a spooky voice.

"I thought they were called the undead," Danny said.

This gave Phobos an idea. "Christina, after supper, may I borrow some paper and a pen?"

"Of course," she said.

Cupid arched a brow, but Phobos said nothing.

Later, while they sat at the table in the shack, bathed in the soft glow of the lantern, Phobos reminded Cupid that tomorrow was the deadline for Ellie to claim her purpose.

"I haven't forgotten," Cupid said. "What's that book you have there?"

"Oh, this? I borrowed it from Jaquelyn. She checked it out from her school library to help her with her English project." Phobos handed it to Cupid.

Cupid read the title aloud: "*The Gods and Goddesses of Ancient Greece.*"

"There's some funny shit in there," Phobos said. "But it's unnerving how much the mortals have gotten right."

"Deimos has probably already read this one, don't you think?"

"I'm sure of it. Don't you have that book in your library, back at the castle?"

Cupid laughed. "I honestly wouldn't know. The books are Psyche's."

"The mortals think that Hypnos and Thanatos are the children of Nyx."

"I wonder what Hades and Persephone think of that," Cupid said with a grin.

"I know. Right? Check out what the book says about Thanatos. Jaquelyn has it bookmarked."

Phobos held his breath as Cupid turned to the page. Phobos had folded a piece of paper into a bookmark. On one side, he wrote. *Give this to Thanatos.* On the other side he wrote: *Bring your father to me.*

Cupid pocketed the bookmark and read a passage of the book aloud: "Thanatos, also known as Orcus and Mors, was the god of Death. The son of Night and twin brother of Hypnos (Sleep), he was believed to be a beautiful young man but, because of his ghastly task, was very unpopular with both man and gods." Cupid chuckled and added, "Well, they got the part right about him being *unpopular.*"

Phobos laughed, too, though it was forced. He was wondering if Cupid understood—really understood—what Phobos wanted him to do.

"When?" Cupid finally asked.

"Tonight," Phobos said.

Just then, they heard a noise outside the door. Cupid jumped to his feet and opened it. Jaquelyn was standing there in the dark with her hand over her mouth.

At the sight of Cupid, she backed away.

Phobos went to the door. "Jaquelyn? What's wrong?"

"I-I didn't mean to eavesdrop."

Phobos exchanged a worried glance with Cupid.

"Are you guys playing a trick on me?"

"Yes!" Phobos said. "I'm sorry. I didn't think it would upset you."

She shook her head. "It wasn't a trick. You didn't know I'd be there, at the door."

"Why *were* you at the door?" Cupid asked suspiciously.

"I needed my book."

"Take it." Cupid held it out to her.

She shook her head and backed away.

"You have nothing to fear from us," Phobos said.

She turned and ran across the pea gravel to the house.

"Do you think she'll tell her parents?" Cupid asked.

"I don't know, but nothing's changed. Got it?"

"I'll be here."

"After tonight, brother, I'll finally be able to forgive you."

Cupid laughed. "It's about damn time."

Ellie awoke with a start. Panic riddled her heart, and she jumped from the bed to the river of fire, where she was sick.

Deimos flew to her side and handed her a towel. "Are you okay?"

"Can I have some water?"

He opened his palm, where a golden goblet filled with ice and water appeared. He handed it to her.

"Thank you," she said before taking a few sips.

She set the goblet on the granite tabletop and collapsed on one of the wooden chairs. She hadn't slept well because of everything Deimos had told her—especially the part about the loyalists' fear that her baby was just as much a threat to Mount Olympus as she was.

He'd said that the babies of deities were mortal until they were born. He'd also said that Zeus and the loyalists were planning to kill her baby while it was still in her womb, and it would be easier for them to do it while she was stripped of her powers on the Garcia family's ranch. He'd said that Zeus and the loyalists had wanted to destroy the baby as soon as they'd heard of its existence, but Artemis had argued that the loss of the baby would be a better punishment for Deimos and Phobos at a later date, after Ellie had begun to show.

For this reason, Deimos and the other rebels didn't believe Zeus would commute Ellie's sentence.

But Deimos had said that if Zeus *did* pardon her on Mount Olympus, Hypnos, who had a power to multiply himself—a power called disintegration, which only one other god, his brother Thanatos, possessed—would turn himself into a massive army while Persephone would take Ellie beneath the protection of the helm and steal away to the Underworld.

Deimos sat across from her at the granite tabletop. "I'm sorry you have to go through this."

"Thank you." She reached across the table and squeezed his hand. "I'm sorry for you, too."

"The plan is going to work," Deimos insisted. "Zeus won't want to pardon you."

"If Phobos knew that he'd screwed up your plans to rescue me, he'd…I don't know what he'd do." She took another sip from the goblet.

"Let's consider the worst-case scenario again," Deimos said. "Suppose Zeus decides *not* to pardon you."

"He'll try to swallow me, right? My baby and I would be stuck in his belly like Athena's mom. What was her name?"

"Metis," Deimos said. "But the rebels won't let that happen. Hypnos will leave the protection of the helm and amass an army. Persephone will be there to hide you and bring you to safety. Have faith. The plan will work."

"Why won't Hades or Persephone use the helm to rescue Phobos and Cupid?" she asked. "Aren't they vulnerable on the ranch without their powers? And poor Phobos has no idea what's become of me."

She couldn't stop thinking of Artemis's last words to Phobos: *And you boys will have to wait to learn her fate when you return in three months. Will she be swallowed by Zeus? Condemned to the Titan Pit? Or will she spend her days and nights in the arms of Deimos? Enjoy your agony, Phobos.*

Ellie shuddered when she imagined Phobos worrying about her and the baby, knowing there was nothing he could do to help them.

"Zeus won't send you back to the ranch if Cupid and Phobos aren't there. Why would he? The whole point of your sentence was to punish me and my brothers. We need *them* there to keep *you* there until the rebels are ready to rescue all three of you."

"And when will that be? And why have they waited so long?"

"We had to wait until after you claimed your purpose, or you'd revert back to a mortal and become an easy target. The only place you can claim your purpose is on Mount Olympus."

"Oh." She took another sip of the water.

"You don't know how scared I was when I heard you say you might not claim one."

"I'm sorry."

Deimos leaned across the table and cupped her cheeks. "I know this hasn't been easy for you, Ellie, but I hope *you* know that the rebels are committed to saving you and the baby."

"Are they?"

"*They're* doing it to save Mount Olympus. *I'm* doing it because I love you like I've never loved another in all my life."

"I love you, too, Deimos." Ellie struggled to keep the panic from her voice. "And I really hope this plan works—for all of our sakes."

CHAPTER TWENTY-TWO

The Rebels

Phobos lay on his bunk with towels under his head and shoulders to catch the blood. He held a nail in his fist and had been clutching it so tightly, that he'd drawn blood from his palm.

Ellie. Hades. Tartarus. Phobos repeated the three names, so he wouldn't forget. He knew all too well, from the many times Deimos had killed him, that a soul becomes disoriented, confused, and forgetful once it leaves its body. Phobos couldn't afford to forget the purpose of his mission.

Ellie. Hades. Tartarus.

Cupid, who sat on a wooden chair beside the bunk, said, "There are more effective ways, you know."

Phobos was grateful that Cupid had chosen his words carefully. If spies were watching, Phobos didn't want them to figure out what he was up to.

But Cupid was right. There were more effective ways. Phobos could use a scythe from the barn to decapitate himself. Death would be instant. However, his body would need days—possibly an entire week—to recover before calling his soul to return. During that time, his body would be vulnerable to his enemies—not to mention the fact that Cupid would be left to shovel dung and spread hay all by his lonesome. Plus, the use of a scythe and decapitation would surely be noticed by spies who might then subvert Phobos's plan.

A nail to the throat would be a slower and more agonizing death as he waited to bleed out, but it would be less conspicuous, particularly since Cupid had agreed to clean Phobos up so he appeared to be sleeping. And the damage to his body, being minimal, should allow Phobos to heal in an hour or two. This should provide enough time for his soul to go to Tartarus and speak with Hades.

But because his soul wouldn't be there long, Phobos needed Cupid to deliver the bookmark with Phobos's message to Thanatos. Even if Thanatos, as he came for Phobos's soul, chose not to reveal himself to Cupid, Cupid was prepared to wave the bookmark over Phobos's body at the moment of death.

Since conceiving of this idea at suppertime, Phobos had been praying to Hades to meet with him in Tartarus, so, even if Thanatos failed to get the message, there was a chance Hades would come.

Phobos felt like his plan was sure to work. The only thing standing in his way was his own cowardice.

At his father's command, Phobos had fought Deimos a hundred times to the death, and Phobos had lost and died at least fifty percent of the time. He wasn't afraid to die. That's not what kept his hand from driving the nail through his throat.

What stayed his hand was his fear of the pain and agony he would endure as he bled out. He'd seen hundreds of thousands of mortals die in this way, and it was always ugly and miserable and grotesque. Even now, he shuddered at what he was about to put himself through. Get it over with, he told himself again and again. Just get it over with.

But his fist continued to clutch the nail.

Ellie stood beside the big, white bed in her guest chambers, where Deimos had helped her to climb into her old, smelly clothes and cowboy boots from the ranch.

"You have to look like you just escaped from the rebels," he reminded her when she made a face.

"Can't Artemis say that my captors bathed and dressed me?"

Deimos laughed. "We don't want to give Zeus any excuse to keep you on Mount Olympus. The smellier and dirtier you are, the more likely he'll send you back."

"Not my hair!" she cried, when Deimos snapped his fingers and replaced her tidy, clean curls with the frizzy mess she'd worn on arrival.

Deimos pushed her hair from her face. "You're still beautiful, Ellie."

"I don't feel beautiful. And the smell of my clothes and hair is making me sick."

"Do you want more crackers?"

"No. I don't think I can eat a thing."

"I wish you'd eaten more. You need your strength."

"I wish I could, Deimos. Believe me. It sucks to be hungry but to not have a decent appetite."

"I'm sorry." He slipped his arms around her waist.

"If only that was the worst of my worries. I should shut up and quit complaining and just be grateful I've made it this far. What if this is the last time I ever see you?"

"It's not, Ellie. Don't think that way."

"Something occurred to me—something we haven't talked about."

"What?"

"What if Zeus stops me from claiming my purpose? What if he finds a way to make me revert to a mortal, so he can kill me and the baby?"

"Artemis won't let that happen. Have faith. Trust the plan."

She took a deep breath and exhaled slowly. As much as she loved Deimos and relied on his support and encouragement, his presence wasn't helping her one bit.

"Ready to go to the throne room to meet up with the others?" he asked.

As she continued to exhale, she nodded.

He took her hand and led her from the room.

Phobos gripped the nail. Beads of sweat had formed on his forehead, and he'd begun to tremble.

Ellie. Hades. Tartarus.

He couldn't afford to forget.

He brought the nail toward his neck but stopped short. He couldn't bring himself to inflict such agonizing pain on himself.

"Bro'," he said to Cupid. "How would you feel about helping a brother out?"

"I was wondering how long it would take you to ask." He stood from his chair, grabbed the nail, and thrust the pointed end into Phobos's neck.

Phobos gasped but didn't cry out, because he didn't want to attract the attention of enemy spies. He clutched his neck as Cupid withdrew the nail and blood spurted, warm and throbbing, down his skin.

Without his powers, everything hurt more—the sharp pain of the nail penetrating his skin, the burn where the air met the open wound, and the dull ache of the arteries and veins as they emptied. Even his bones and muscles ached.

Cupid used the towels to mop up the blood, but it was so much more than Phobos had expected, and soon it was necessary to use the bedding from the top bunk.

Phobos wanted to say something funny to Cupid, to make him laugh, but he'd waited too late. Blood choked him, and when he tried to breathe, it felt like he was sucking in fire and sand.

"I'll see you soon, brother," Cupid said. "Sleep well."

Phobos felt like he was falling—falling and spinning. When he opened his eyes again, Thanatos was there, pulling him from the bed. Phobos couldn't recall where he was or what was happening, but he knew there was something important he must do. When Thanatos took a piece of folded paper, the size of a bookmark, from Cupid's outstretched hand, Phobos remembered.

Ellie. Hades. Tartarus.

Thanatos said nothing as they flew from the ranch in Texas across the night sky. They crossed over the Pacific Ocean and headed toward Greece in time to see Helios arrive in his golden cup, bringing dawn to the east.

Soon they plunged toward the earth and into a deep and narrow chasm. Thanatos flew expertly through the turns and bends, having flown the route for centuries with billions of other souls. They emerged in the foggy cavernous Underworld where the Acheron met the Styx and where Charon, the old ferryman, was waiting.

When he stepped onto the boat, Phobos was confused. Where was he? What was happening?

"Thanatos?" Phobos asked. "Where are you taking me?"

"To Tartarus."

There was something important Phobos wanted to do in Tartarus. What was it? It was on the tip of his tongue.

As the boat sailed past Cerberus and through the tall iron gates, Thanatos said, "You've come to meet with my father."

"Oh, yeah. Ellie. Hades. Tartarus."

Charon took a right at the House of Judgment and sailed down the River Styx before stopping abruptly at the gate to Tartarus.

"This way," Thanatos said, leading him along the flames of the Phlegethon and into the room of torture.

"Have a seat," Thanatos said of the rocky ledge along one wall. "I'll let my father know that you're here."

Ellie. Hades. Tartarus.

Artemis, Persephone, and a younger god, who looked to be the same age as Deimos, were waiting for Ellie as she entered the Underworld.

"Where's Lord Hades?" Deimos asked as he followed Ellie into the room.

Ellie covered her mouth and yawned.

Artemis frowned. "You'll have to show more self-control on Mount Olympus, if you don't want to give Hypnos away."

Ellie bit her lip. The desire to yawn and to close her eyes was strong with the god of sleep so close.

"Hi, there," the young god said. His blue eyes were as radiant as those of Deimos and Phobos, but his hair was blond. "You can call me Hip."

"It's nice to meet you, Hip," Ellie said, as she stifled another yawn.

"It'll be hard to resist sleep without your powers," Persephone said, "but not impossible, since you're one of us now."

"I'll try my best to keep my distance," Hip said, taking a few paces away from Ellie.

"Hades will be here shortly," Persephone said to Deimos. "He was summoned to Tartarus by your brother."

"My brother?" Deimos's eyes widened. "Which one?"

"Phobos," Persephone said.

Ellie's mouth fell open. "How? Have his powers been restored?"

"No," Artemis said. "He must have killed himself."

Ellie turned to Deimos. "But why? Why would he do that?"

"To check on you," Deimos said. "It was actually a brilliant idea. Don't tell him I said so. It'll go to his head."

"How can you speak so flippantly right now?" Artemis asked Deimos.

"He's trying to keep me calm," Ellie snapped at Artemis.

"And it's obviously not working," Artemis snapped back.

"Where's Pasithea when you need her?" Hip murmured.

"Don't you dare pray to her, Hypnos!" Artemis snapped at him. "She's a loyalist!"

"It was a joke. Lighten up," Hip said.

Ellie decided she liked the god of sleep.

"Thank you," he said with a wink.

Ugh! She'd done that thing again where she'd accidentally prayed. She gave Deimos a worried glance.

"You'll do fine," Deimos said, as he squeezed her hand. Then he asked the others, "Where's Psyche? I thought she would be here, too."

"She's with Cupid, watching over Phobos's body," Persephone replied.

"Are we ready, then?" Artemis asked the group.

"Let's give Hades a few more minutes," Persephone said. "He won't be long, and he may have some parting words for us."

"How dare you summon me in my own kingdom!" Hades snarled outside the gate to Tartarus.

Phobos had forgotten what an ass the god of the Underworld could be—*all* the gods could be. Phobos supposed he should include himself among them. He'd been an ass more times than he could count.

"My apologies, Lord Hades. I've come to learn the fate of Ellie Beaufort, at my own peril. My body lies vulnerable while I'm here, seeking information. Do you know where she is?"

"Silence, you idiot!" Hades entered the gate and looked as though he might wring Phobos by the neck. "Don't presume you're the only one who came to Tartarus seeking information about the rebels."

Phobos glanced around the torture room. It stretched further than he could see in both directions. Not far from him were slabs of stone with souls strapped to them. One of the Furies seemed to be conducting an interrogation. Opposite them, a soul slumped on a nearby rock sat resting its chin in its hand.

Phobos suddenly recognized the soul. It was Hermes.

Phobos turned to Hades with wide eyes.

Hades lowered his voice. "We intercepted Artemis and her prisoner when they left the ranch. We had Ellie for a while, but Artemis managed to free her. They escaped moments ago, and they're headed to Mount Olympus."

Even though he had no body—and therefore no actual tear ducts—Phobos wanted to weep.

"We recovered the helm, however," Hades said. "Thanks to you. And that allowed me the satisfaction of throwing my spear into Artemis's back—the loyalist scum."

Before Phobos could ask another question, Hades swiftly took his leave.

Ellie's legs were numb by the time the lord of the Underworld returned from his meeting with Phobos in Tartarus. She wanted to ask how Phobos was, but she held her tongue. Hades appeared to be in no mood to answer questions.

He carried a spear where he stood on the dais before his throne. "There's no time to lose. Is everyone ready?"

"We were waiting on you," Artemis said.

Hades pointed a finger at the huntress. "Make certain that every word you say is true. We can't afford to be compromised by your brother."

"I've been his sister for centuries," Artemis said. "I know how to handle him."

Persephone flew to her husband's side and kissed his cheek. "We've got this, darling. We'll return shortly."

Ellie suddenly realized that Hades wasn't angry. He was scared. His wife and son were going into harm's way while he remained behind to protect his realm.

"Good luck, then," Hades said.

Deimos gave Ellie a nod of encouragement. Then Artemis grabbed Ellie's arm and turned to go.

Ellie flinched when Artemis cried out in pain. Hades had thrown his spear into the huntress's back, and it protruded from her chest.

"That will make your story more believable," Hades said.

<u>CHAPTER TWENTY-THREE</u>

Mount Olympus

Phobos wandered over to Hermes not long after Hades had left Tartarus.

"What are you doing here, cousin?" Phobos asked.

"When I suggested that the gods needed to work together, my father sliced off my head."

"Wow. Sounds like Father of the Year material."

"You bet. Just before he wielded his sword against me, he called me a rebel sympathizer."

"Are you?"

"I don't like gods warring with gods. I meant it when I said we should work together to solve the riddle of Ellie Beaufort."

"Zeus refuses to listen to any opinion that isn't his own," Phobos pointed out. "You can't blame Hades for taking action."

"Unfortunately, he and the rebels don't stand a chance on Mount Olympus," Hermes said. "Zeus has thought of everything, and there are traps in waiting for any play Hades intends to make."

"I hope you're wrong, cousin," Phobos said.

"So, what brings you to Tartarus?" Hermes asked.

"I'm still in love with Ellie," he admitted. "Artemis took her, and I was hoping to learn from Hades what had become of her."

"I'm fairly certain that Artemis has defected to the rebel cause."

"But Hades said…"

"That was for my benefit. He thinks I'm a spy."

"Are you?"

Hermes shrugged. "I've shared information with both sides."

"Playing both sides? Sounds shady."

"Only trying to end the conflict, Phobos. You can keep your judgment to yourself."

"You're right. Sorry, man. I didn't mean to be an ass."

"That's okay, cousin. I'm used to that by now."

They shared a laugh.

Phobos had just begun to worry that something horrible had happened to his body when it finally called to him. "Looks like I'm done here. See you later."

"See you," Hermes said.

Of its own accord, the soul of Phobos flew through air and objects along the shortest route to where his body still lay in the bottom bunk in the shack.

When he opened his eyes, he was shocked by what he saw: His parents stood beside Cupid and Psyche, who wore adamantine shackles and chains around their necks, wrists, and ankles. His mother had tears streaming down her cheeks.

Phobos sat up and discovered that he, too, had been shackled.

"What's going on?" Phobos asked.

"Sorry, son," Ares said. "We're taking you as our prisoners to Mount Olympus."

Ellie closed her eyes against the brightness of the early morning light as she flew on the end of Artemis's arm from the narrow chasm of the Underworld. When her eyes adjusted, she saw Artemis's blood had sprayed all over Ellie's clothes. The metallic smell of blood mixed with the earthy one of dung made Ellie sick over Greece.

"Hold yourself together," Artemis snapped.

Knowing the goddess was in pain, Ellie held her tongue. She wiped her mouth and glanced back, where Persephone and Hypnos were supposed to be following; however, the protection of the helm rendered them invisible. Ellie would have to trust on faith that they were there.

It took them less than five minutes to fly from the palace of Hades and Persephone to the gates of Mount Olympus. Artemis commanded the seasons to open the gates. The roar of thunder—as loud as a train—was followed by a brief shower. Then the clouds parted, revealing a rainbow. Artemis grabbed Ellie's arm once again and flew through the gates.

Artemis dripped blood on the golden pavers of the courtyard and the rainbow steps leading to the entrance of the grand temple. When they reached the great hall, Artemis flung Ellie onto the marble floor and fell from the air to her knees. Ellie wondered if Artemis had fallen for dramatic effect, or if she was truly suffering from the injury caused by Hades's spear.

Zeus and Hera stood from their thrones. Some of the other gods gasped. Ellie was shocked to see Ares and Aphrodite near Hera with three prisoners in white shackles and chains: Psyche, Cupid, and Phobos.

"Phobos!" Ellie cried.

She wanted to go to him, but she remembered that she had a role to play, and her part wouldn't come until after Artemis spoke.

"Where have you been?" Zeus shouted at Artemis. "We expected you yesterday."

Panting, Artemis said, "After I left the ranch with Ellie, Persephone confronted me and took the helm. She's joined the rebels. My prisoner was taken into their custody. I managed to retrieve Ellie from the Underworld today but not before Hades impaled me with his spear."

"And what of the helm?" Ares asked.

"I don't have it," Artemis said.

Zeus turned to Apollo. "Does your sister speak the truth?"

"She does," Apollo declared.

Zeus stepped down from the dais onto the floor before Artemis and Ellie. Ellie had climbed to her feet and stood at Artemis's side, but the huntress was still on her knees, panting.

It had been three months since Ellie had last stood in this temple, which was open to the blue sky above. Phobos had once told her that the sun always shone on Mount Olympus, even when Helios was on the other side of the world. The room was in the shape of an oval with a double throne in the center back, where Zeus and Hera stood. On either side of the double throne were five more thrones along the perimeter of the room, each raised on a dais about a foot high from the marble floor, and all but four were occupied by a god or goddess. Ellie supposed one of the empty thrones belonged to Artemis and another to Aphrodite. Another might belong to Demeter, who was away at her winter cabin. Ellie had no idea about the fourth.

"Father," said the gray-eyed goddess to Zeus's right.

"Yes, Athena?" he replied.

"Artemis said that her prisoner was taken into custody by the rebels but didn't say whether she had been as well."

"That's true," Aphrodite said. "If Artemis *wasn't* being held by the rebels, where *was* she?"

"Were you taken prisoner?" Zeus asked Artemis.

"No," Artemis said.

"Then why didn't you return here to inform me of Ellie's status?" Zeus demanded.

"I spent my time trying to recover her," Artemis said.

Zeus glanced at Apollo.

Apollo shook his head.

Ellie saw the color spread across Artemis's cheeks. Zeus knew the huntress was lying.

As Zeus glowered down at Artemis, Ellie wondered if Persephone and Hypnos were making any progress in their mission to rescue Hecate.

"Phobos coerced me into speaking on Ellie's behalf," Artemis added. "I swore an oath for the helm. To keep my oath, I ask that you pardon Ellie Beaufort and commute her sentence to the three months she's already served."

Ellie held her breath, anxious to hear Zeus's reply.

"I see no reason to send her back," Zeus declared. "I hereby commute Ellie Beaufort's sentence to the three months she's already served."

Ellie glanced at Phobos and Cupid, wishing she could hear their thoughts.

"You don't seem happy about the pardon," Zeus said to Ellie.

"I've had my share of shit, Lord Zeus," Ellie answered boldly.

She hadn't expected to make the deities in the room laugh. Even Artemis chuckled from where she knelt at Ellie's side.

Ellie glanced again at Phobos, who gave her a solemn smile. Then he mouthed something to her, but she couldn't read his lips. It may have been, "I'm your precious," but that seemed like an odd thing for him to say.

The smell of Artemis's blood made Ellie queasy again. She clutched her stomach and tried to remain calm.

"If your pregnancy pains you, I can remedy that," Zeus said in a voice that wasn't unkind.

"I *want* this baby," Ellie insisted.

"Bab*ies*," Hera said.

Ellie glanced again at Phobos, who wore a look of surprise that must have mirrored her own.

"Bab*ies*?" Phobos repeated.

"Twins," Hera said. "Girls."

Ellie held her belly and smiled with glee. She was having twin girls!

"Congratulations," Hera said coldly.

Ellie wanted to ask about the father, but she held her tongue, fearing that Phobos might be destroyed by the answer.

"Can we refrain from the unnecessary cruelty?" a god seated across the room cried out.

Ellie didn't recognize him. He was less beautiful than the other gods, with a slight hunch in his back, but still attractive by human standards.

"Is there something you wish to say, Hephaestus?" Zeus asked.

"I agree that we have no choice but to kill or imprison this girl, since she poses a threat to our way of life," Hephaestus said. "But there's no reason to add to her pain and suffering. Stop taunting the poor thing and get on with it."

Artemis climbed to her feet, holding the head of the spear that still jutted through her chest. "Ellie has come to Mount Olympus to claim her purpose."

Knowing that was her cue, Ellie opened her mouth to speak, only to be interrupted by Zeus.

"What do we have here?" he demanded as two goddesses with wings emerged from a door behind one of the empty thrones.

The goddesses held Hypnos beneath a golden fisherman's net that seemed to have the ability to incapacitate him. Ellie scanned the room for signs of Persephone, hoping that the queen of the underworld had managed to remain undetected. Was it possible that she could still save Hecate without help from the god of sleep? Or was the rebel mission already doomed?

Phobos watched in silence as the events unfolded on Mount Olympus—events he was helpless to change. He was still reeling with the news of the twin girls when Hip appeared beneath Poseidon's golden net between Nike and Iris. This could only mean that Hip had been working for the rebels and had failed.

For the hundredth time, Phobos prayed to his parents to come to their senses and to come to the aid of their children, but if Ares or Aphrodite heard him, neither acted on it.

Phobos wondered if he and his brother would have been waking up right about now to the morning bell and, shortly after, grooming the horses, if Phobos hadn't been determined to go to Tartarus by killing himself.

And he was anxious that Ellie had still not yet claimed her purpose. He worried that Zeus had been stalling, to make Ellie run out of time and revert to a mortal, so Zeus could kill her and the babies.

Moments ago, he'd been unsuccessful in communicating it to her by mouthing, "Claim your purpose," so he prayed to her, even though he knew she couldn't hear him without her powers.

Zeus turned to Hypnos. "I should have known that a son of Hades would prove a traitor. Like father like son."

"I could say the same of you, Lord Zeus," Hypnos spat.

"How dare you speak to me that way! Everything I do is for the protection of Mount Olympus!"

"You mean to save yourself by swallowing Ellie, like your father tried to swallow you," Hip said through the golden net.

Zeus's complexion turned as red as liquid lava.

Poseidon shouted, "Are you here alone, Hypnos? Or is someone here with you, beneath your father's helm?"

Hypnos refused to reply.

Athena paced around the room, as though she hoped to discover a traitor beneath the helm.

"What was your purpose in coming here today?" Zeus asked.

"Are you here to free Ellie?" Ares shouted.

Suddenly, Ellie shocked everyone in the room when she shouted, "I claim my purpose! I am the goddess of lost causes!"

Immediately, the luminosity returned to her skin, and she became taller and more muscular and even more beautiful, which Phobos would have thought impossible. Phobos was relieved but still worried that Zeus would open his mouth and swallow her.

In fact, Zeus seemed to have that very thing on his mind as he stormed across the room toward Ellie.

But Ellie surprised Zeus—and Phobos—when she yanked the spear from Artemis's chest and hurled it at Nike, who was then penned against the wooden door. Zeus paused with surprise as Artemis shot off two arrows to take down Iris, which allowed someone hiding beneath the helm to lift the golden net and free Hypnos.

Even angrier and redder than before, Zeus raged toward Ellie. Ellie dodged him by sliding along the marble floor, like a runner sliding into home base, and by kicking his legs out from under him with her cowboy boots.

As Zeus flew up and recovered, the god of sleep disintegrated into an army of dozens. Hip attacked each of the loyalists, three to one, as Artemis shot off more arrows, including one that hit Zeus in the shoulder.

Ellie flew to Phobos, who, along with Cupid and Psyche, had been abandoned by his parents in the battle. Ellie tried with all her might to rip the chains from them.

"They're too strong," Phobos said. "Let's get out of here."

Phobos knew that if any version of Hip were to be fatally wounded, the entire army would be lost.

C H A P T E R   T W E N T Y - F O U R

Prisoners

As Ellie fled with Phobos, Cupid, and Psyche from the great hall, they were stopped at the rainbow steps by gray-eyed Athena. Psyche flew up in her chains and shackles and taunted Athena, apparently hoping to distract the other goddess, so Ellie could get Cupid and Phobos to safety.

However, Athena didn't fall for it. She drew her sword and attacked Ellie.

Without a weapon of her own, Ellie's only recourse was to dodge Athena's blows. Ellie pretended that she was going in one direction only to fly in another—a strategy she used when stealing bases or faking out the pitcher. When Athena sliced her sword through the air in Ellie's direction, Ellie slid along the gold pavers, using the same move she'd used to elude Zeus. Then Ellie hopped in the air and scanned the courtyard for a weapon.

Finding none, Ellie flew in the direction of the stables. As she did, she heard an urgent prayer from Persephone:

Leave the prisoners and meet me at the gates alone. We'll come back for the others.

But there was no way in hell Ellie would leave Phobos and Cupid in their vulnerable states in the hands of Zeus and his loyalists. And who knew what they would do to Psyche?

I'm not leaving without them, Ellie prayed to Persephone.

Persephone replied: *Hypnos has been fatally wounded. Artemis and I must get him and Hecate home. We can't wait for you.*

Go! Ellie said as she scrambled from Athena in the stables, hoping to find a pitchfork, a rope, a brush—anything.

The only thing she found was Pegasus.

Ellie climbed on his back and commanded him to fly. Instead, Pegasus reared back on his hind legs and shrieked. Athena had them cornered, and Pegasus refused to advance.

Making to slide toward Athena's feet, Ellie waited for Athena to fly down before Ellie raced through the ceiling of the stables and returned to the rainbow steps in search of Phobos, Cupid, and Psyche. But when she reached the entrance to the temple, Psyche and the brothers were nowhere in sight. Ellie flew into the great hall, where Zeus and his loyalists—save Athena—had returned to their thrones to rest and to gloat.

They were gloating because they knew they had her. The other rebels were gone, and still shackled and chained in the center of the room were Phobos, Cupid, and Psyche.

"No!" Phobos groaned.

She supposed the sight of her had dashed his hopes that she had somehow managed to escape.

"Welcome back," Zeus said with a smug grin. He held a golden goblet—all the gods held them. "I'd like to toast the loyalists for a fine victory today." He raised his goblet and said, "Cheers!"

Athena flew past Ellie and returned to her throne. A goblet appeared in her hand in time for her to say, "Cheers!" with the others.

Ellie continued to scan her surroundings for a weapon—anything that could get her and her loved ones out of this mess. Finding none, she walked across the marble floor toward Phobos, Cupid, and Psyche and said, "I'll give myself up if you release the other prisoners."

Zeus threw his head back and laughed. Many of the other gods did, too.

"She thinks she has a leg to stand on," Poseidon said through his chuckles.

"Cheeky girl," Athena said.

"I'm the one you want," Ellie said. "You win. You got me. Why won't you let them go? What threat are Cupid and Phobos to you without their powers anyway?" She glowered at Ares. "They're your *sons!*" She turned to Aphrodite. "*Your* sons!" To Zeus and Hera, she added, "And your *grandsons!*" To the others she said, "They're your nephews, your cousins, your *family!*"

"They're leverage," Zeus said. "They stay imprisoned until the threat is neutralized, until the rebels have no reason to attack again."

"The rebels don't care about *them!*" Ellie insisted. "The rebels are just like you! They only care about themselves. They only want to save me because they think it will change the prophecy and spare Mount Olympus."

"That's probably true," Poseidon said.

"I had a chance to leave with the rebels at the gate," Ellie said. "They told me to leave Phobos, Cupid, and Psyche behind. It doesn't sound to me like these prisoners give you any leverage."

Zeus glanced at Apollo, who nodded.

"She's quite dramatic, isn't she?" Hera said coldly.

"Entertaining, too," Poseidon added.

"Enough with the taunting," Hephaestus said. "Let the girl have her moment, so we can get on with it."

Ellie gave Hephaestus a grateful nod. "I'd say that if I don't have a leg to stand on, then the threat *is* neutralized. That leaves you with no reason to keep the prisoners."

"She should have gone to law school," Apollo said.

"Let them go," Ellie pleaded, "so Phobos doesn't have to see you swallow the woman he loves, along with the babies that may or may not be his. Can't you spare him that unnecessary pain?"

"I don't intend to swallow you, my dear," Zeus said in his patronizing way. "Not yet. We want to better understand the prophecy before we decide what to do with you. Meanwhile, you'll be our prisoner."

"Fine. I'll be your prisoner. But let them go. Send them back to the ranch. Strip Psyche of her powers and send her with them."

Psyche shook her head and lifted her brows at Ellie, apparently not pleased with Ellie's idea. Then she prayed: *Don't encourage them to render me useless.*

I'm trying to get you out of here, Ellie replied to Psyche.

Thanks, but no thanks, Psyche prayed in return.

"That's not a bad idea," Aphrodite said. "We should strip Psyche of her powers and send her with the boys to finish their sentences. Perhaps, by the time they return with their powers, this little matter will be all cleared up."

"Hear, hear," Ares said. "It will keep them out of the way."

"Hmm," Zeus began. "We have a motion and a second. All in favor?"

The room resounded with "I."

"Then it's settled," Zeus said. "Psyche, I hereby relieve you of your powers."

Ellie was grateful for this small victory, even though the looks on the faces of Psyche and Phobos told her they felt differently. She could hear their prayers, asking how she could send them away. She wished they could hear hers.

Only Cupid's prayers to her were reassuring: *This was the right move, Ellie, even if my wife and brother don't see it.*

As the luminosity in Psyche's skin faded, the goddess glared at Ellie.

"Since Artemis has defected, I need someone else to escort these prisoners to the ranch and to keep an eye on them as they finish out their sentence," Zeus said.

"I volunteer," Aphrodite said. "I want to restore my children's dignity in the eyes of this court as soon as possible. I'll see to it that they do as they're told."

"Very well," Zeus said. "Take them."

Hera stood from her throne. "Before you go, Aphrodite, I believe Phobos might be interested in knowing more about the twins Ellie is carrying." Hera turned to Phobos. "Would you, Phobos?"

Ellie clutched her abdomen, praying to Hera not to torment him if Deimos is the father.

Phobos closed his eyes and opened them again. "Why not, Hera? Hit me with it."

"Perhaps you should hold off revealing that information," Zeus said to his wife.

"Fine," Hera said, apparently not pleased.

"Tell, me, Hera," Phobos asked with a hint of desperation. "Are they mine?"

Hera honored her husband's request and refused to reply.

"Better take the chariot," Zeus said to Aphrodite as she left her throne to retrieve her prisoners.

Tears slid down Ellie's cheeks as she watched Aphrodite lead Phobos and the others away. Ellie was happy that Phobos was free from Mount Olympus but terrified that she might never see him again.

As Aphrodite drove the chariot over the Pacific Ocean toward Texas, Phobos seethed while Cupid attempted to console his weeping wife.

"You're on the wrong side of this, Mother," Cupid said. "I'm not saying that because I expect you to turn around and take us back. I felt bad for leaving the Garcia family just when they needed me the most. I want to return. I really do. But that doesn't change the fact that you are wrong in this."

"You're welcome to your own opinion," Aphrodite said. "And I'm welcome to mine."

"Base your opinions on logic rather than on fear," Phobos said to his mother.

Aphrodite laughed. "How ironic, coming from you!"

"You should consider me an expert in this matter," Phobos insisted. "I've seen, firsthand, what fear can do to people."

Aphrodite scoffed. "You yourself have shown the good that fear can do."

"But not when it directly counters logic," Psyche said. "That's what Phobos is trying to say. Hades represents logic. Zeus represents fear."

"Choose the side of logic, Mother," Cupid said.

"Everything that Hades has said is hypothetical," Aphrodite pointed out. "Apollo has had visions."

"Which are given to him by the Fates," Phobos argued. "If the Fates are testing us, they might be manipulating the visions."

"Only the Fates know for certain what the future holds," Cupid added. "You can't rely on bits and pieces that a few seers have described. They mean nothing."

"Nothing," Aphrodite mocked, shaking her head. "Apollo saw the columns of Mount Olympus crumbling. That means something."

"You should do what you know in your heart is right, regardless of the outcome," Psyche said. "To me, it's crystal clear. You don't kill innocent people. I can't see how the Fates would punish a pantheon for taking the high moral ground. On the other hand, I can see…"

"Oh, stop with your self-righteous blubbering!" Aphrodite said, cutting Psyche off.

Cupid stroked his wife's hair as she wept against his shoulder.

"For the goddess of love," Phobos said, "you sure carry around a lot of hate."

"Speak for yourself," Aphrodite spat. "I saw the cruel way you treated Ellie during those first weeks on the ranch."

"He'd just been pierced with an arrow of hate," Cupid said.

"Ellie is carrying *your* granddaughters," Phobos said to his mother. "I think you could learn a thing or two about love from Christina Garcia."

"Enough!" Aphrodite shrieked.

The instant Phobos had made the comment to shame his mother, he regretted it. Knowing Aphrodite's jealous and vindictive ways, he wouldn't put it past her to hurt or kill Christina and her granddaughters because of Phobos's words.

"If you do anything to hurt the Garcia family, Mother," Phobos said. "I'll never forgive you. I swear on the River Styx that I'll never forgive you."

"Nor will I," Cupid said.

Aphrodite glowered at them but said nothing.

When they reached the Garcia family's ranch in southwest Texas, dawn had just arrived. Aphrodite used a key to remove their adamantine shackles and gave Psyche a bag of clothes, boots, and toiletries. Then, without another word, she dropped them off at the entrance from the south fence and drove away.

Cupid carried Psyche's bag as they hobbled along the dirt road, exhausted from the ordeal they'd just been put through. Christina must have seen them from the farmhouse, for she ran out, still in her apron, to meet them halfway.

"We were so worried!" she said as she hugged each brother. "When you didn't come to breakfast, we went looking for you! You just disappeared!"

"Our parents came and got us in the middle of the night," Phobos said. "Long story."

"I'm just glad you're safe," Christina said. "And who is this beautiful thing?"

"This is my wife, Psyche," Cupid said. "She's come to help in Ellie's place."

"It's nice to meet you, Psyche," Christina said. "What an interesting name. I bet Cupid is glad to be reunited with you. He missed you so much."

"Thank you," Psyche said.

As they continued their walk toward the farmhouse, Christina said, "Danny has already gone out on Chestnut to check on the calves. Jaquelyn stayed home today to groom and clean the stalls."

"I'm sorry we left without saying anything," Phobos said.

"You owe us *nothing*, Phobos. We're so grateful for your help, but you're not obligated to stay."

"We want to help through winter, as promised," Cupid said.

"Well, we appreciate that more than words can say. But tell me, is there any news about Ellie and her family?"

"That's what brought our family out here," Cupid said. "They wanted to give us an update."

"Please tell me it's good news."

Phobos heaved a sigh. "I wish I could."

"Oh, no," Christina said. "What happened?"

Phobos hadn't had time to come up with a reasonable story for the Garcia family and felt at a loss. He was grateful when his brother answered.

"Since she's a celebrity, we're not allowed to talk about it," Cupid said. "Her family doesn't want it in the media."

"I'd never say anything," Christina said. "You should know you can trust me by now, *mijo*."

"We know," Phobos said.

"Someone has kidnapped Ellie," Cupid said. "We don't know if it's a crazy fan or someone from a rival softball team, but they've been threatening her and her family for some time now."

"Oh, my God!" Christina said.

"We didn't know it at the time, but Artemis brought us here to keep Ellie safe," Phobos said.

"Now it all makes sense!" Christina said. "And then we took her to Night in Ol' Del Rio! Oh, no! We blew her cover!"

"It's not your fault," Psyche said. "You couldn't have known."

"I'll ask my church congregation to pray for her safe return, and I promise to pray a rosary for her every night until she's home."

"Thank you," Phobos said.

Rose and Violet were standing on the front porch, waving and jumping up and down.

"Please don't tell the girls," Phobos said.

"No, of course not," Christina agreed.

As they reached the farmhouse, the two little girls hugged each of Phobos's legs. He felt a lump in his throat as he imagined his own twin girls greeting him as he returned home to Ellie one day. It was only a fantasy, but it made him smile.

"We thought you left us!" Rose said. "Where did you go?"

"Their parents needed to see them," Christina said. "But, look! Cupid's wife is here to help, too! Her name is Psyche. Can you say hello?"

"Hello," Rose said.

"Hello," Psyche said.

"Are you hungry?" Christina asked. "I'd be happy to make you some eggs."

"That sounds great," Phobos said. "Thank you."

"Afterwards, we'll help Jaquelyn with the stalls," Cupid said.

"And then crash," Phobos said. "None of us slept last night."

"Poor things," Christina said. "Let's get some food in your bellies."

Christina opened the door, and they followed her inside. Phobos hoped his mother was watching. He prayed to her: *This is what families should look like. This is what love looks like. Why can't you support your sons and at least consider what Hades has to say?*

He doubted his words affected Aphrodite as he sat at the family table, across from the little girls, and entertained them while Christina fried eggs.

CHAPTER TWENTY-FIVE

Escape

These shackles and chains are made of adamantine," Hera said, as she locked them onto Ellie's wrists and ankles, while Ellie sat on the sofa in Demeter's room.

"Not even Zeus can break free of them," the winged goddess named Nike said.

When Hera shot Nike a threatening look, the other winged goddess, named Iris, added, "Not that anyone would ever bind Zeus."

"The shackles and chains can't prevent you from flying," Hera said, "but they make it impossible for you to god-travel or to draw a weapon."

"Besides, the seasons have been ordered to let no one in or out but those specifically authorized by Zeus," Nike added.

"Goodie," Ellie said. "Please tell me you have Netflix."

Hera scowled. "You can be sassy, can't you? But I could tell you something about your babies that would humble you."

Ellie clutched her abdomen and was suddenly queasy. Was Hera merely taunting her, or did she sense something wrong with the twins? Ellie decided she couldn't believe whatever Hera had to say, but she still wanted to hear it.

"Tell me. Please."

"I'll think about it," Hera said. "Meanwhile, Nike and Iris will be keeping an eye on you."

"Why do you hate me so much?" Ellie asked as tears pricked her eyes.

Hera frowned. "It's nothing personal, dear. When a poisonous spider happens to cross my path, it's nothing personal when I squash it, either."

Ellie bit her tongue as Hera flew to the door.

"I'll have Hestia bring you something to eat," Hera said.

Ellie wondered why she would bother but didn't ask as the queen of the Olympians left the room.

Not long after Hera left, while Iris and Nike entertained themselves with a game of cards at a nearby table, the goddess named Hestia entered with a platter of fruits, crackers, cheeses, cakes, and honey, along with a goblet filled with nectar.

"Thank you," Ellie said, her appetite suddenly restored. "Everything looks delicious."

Hestia said nothing. She was neither friendly nor rude. She delivered the tray and left.

Sometime later, after Ellie had eaten and had stretched on the couch and napped, she was awakened by another visitor. He wore the helm and had a finger to his lips. She'd seen this god before and was trying to recall his name.

He prayed to her: *My name is Hermes, and I'm here to rescue you. Do not move a muscle. Close your eyes and pretend to be asleep.*

She did as he asked but wondered how he would manage her rescue with Nike and Iris in the room and the other gods hanging around in the great hall, waiting for this very move.

Then he prayed: *I'm the fastest god alive. No one can catch me. But you'll need to hold on tight.*

In the next instant, they were flying from the room, and everything was a blur, even with goddess vision.

When they finally stopped, Ellie, still clinging to the god's neck, caught her breath and glanced around to get her bearings. Hermes was standing on top of the turret of a castle overlooking the sea on one side and a city on the other. Ellie was about to ask where they were, when Hermes put a finger to his lips.

She prayed: *Where are we?*

Edinburgh, Scotland.

Why? she prayed.

You'll soon see, he replied as he carried her to a strange-looking chariot.

The chariot was golden, like those Ellie had seen driven by other gods, but its wheels were thicker, and it had no horses. Hephaestus, the god with the slight hunchback, sat on the bench seat behind a series of levers and switches. Hermes stepped aboard and seated Ellie between him and the other god.

Hephaestus pulled back a lever, and the chariot flew from the turret into the sky over the North Atlantic Ocean.

As they passed over an enormous island, Ellie prayed to Hermes, *What's the name of that island below?*

Iceland.

My god, where are you taking me?

Just a little bit further.

Ellie was trying to remember her world geography. She knew they were flying north, toward the Arctic, but she couldn't recall what was around Iceland.

She prayed to Hephaestus: *Are we headed to Canada?*

Greenland, Hephaestus said. *To a cave on Mont Forel—Selene's cave. You'll be safe there—I hope.*

Ellie remembered Selene's cave. Beneath the protection of the helm, Ellie, Phobos, and Deimos had tried to sneak a ride aboard the moon goddess's silver chariot. They'd been caught when Ellie had accidentally prayed to Selene. Although the moon goddess had been suspicious of them, she'd released them after checking their story with Hecate, who was her friend.

Those were the days when Phobos and Deimos had been willing to share her. They'd made out with her in the cave until Selene returned and interrupted them. Ellie missed those days.

Why are you helping me? Ellie asked Hephaestus.

Because it's the right thing to do.

Then she prayed to Hermes with the same question.

He replied: *Because I'm a sucker for damsels in distress, especially pregnant ones.*

The chariot descended toward a snow-covered mountain peak near the coast of Greenland. Hephaestus drove to the mouth of Selene's cave, where they hovered in the air until Deimos appeared and waved them inside.

When the chariot came to a stop just inside the cave, Ellie flew into the arms of Deimos. Hermes and Hephaestus didn't stay. Still under the protection of the helm, they left as quickly as they'd arrived.

"Ellie!" Deimos cried, as he held her in his arms. Then he kissed her and stroked her hair. "I'm so relieved to see you!"

"You can't possibly be as relieved as I am! I thought Zeus was going to swallow me!"

"Come and sit down by the fire," Deimos said. "And I'll catch you up on all that's happened since you were captured."

She sat on the sofa before the cozy fire. "I still can't believe I was rescued!"

As she glanced across the room, she was surprised to see someone else, covered by a quilt, sleeping on another sofa, perpendicular to hers. It wasn't Selene's sleeping lover—whom Ellie had seen the last time she'd visited Selene's cave. He was still lying on the bed at the back of the cave, where she'd seen him before.

"Who's that?" Ellie asked Deimos.

"Hecate," Deimos replied. "She's still recovering from Zeus's lightning bolt."

Ellie jumped from the couch and went to Hecate.

Hecate looked up at Ellie.

"Can you move? Can you speak?"

"I speak," Hecate said. "But can't lift my head."

"Not yet," Deimos said as he moved to Ellie's side. "But she's making progress. Do you need more nectar, Hecate?"

"No," the goddess replied. "Rest."

Hecate closed her eyes and appeared to go to sleep.

Ellie and Deimos returned to the other couch. Deimos took her in his arms again and kissed her.

Ellie spoke softly, so as not to awaken Hecate, when she asked, "Wouldn't she be safer in the Underworld?"

"Hades anticipates an attack. That's the first place the loyalists will look for you."

Ellie shuddered.

Deimos kissed her hand. "Don't blame yourself. None of this is your fault."

"Did you hear about Phobos, Cupid, and Psyche?"

Deimos nodded. "You were right to convince Zeus to send them back. Phobos and Cupid are safer there until their powers are restored."

Ellie thought about the three of them, grooming the horses, shoveling dung, and spreading hay, and she felt a strange pang of jealousy. It had been hard work for Ellie, but she'd felt good about finishing a hard day's work. She'd grown to love the horses and the cows—even the pigs. She hoped Deimos the cat was still getting along with the dogs and the chickens.

She'd also grown to love the Garcia family—almost as much as she loved her own. She'd miss them, especially Jaquelyn, whom she'd come to consider a good friend.

But as she thought about the ranch, it was Phobos that her heart missed most of all. She wished it was she, and not Psyche, back on the ranch. Ellie longed to be with Phobos.

Why couldn't she be content in the arms of Deimos? She loved him, too. She ran her fingers through his vibrant hair and kissed him again, grateful that he was here with her, that they could finally be together.

"Now tell me," Ellie said. "How did Hermes break into Mount Olympus with the helm? I was told the seasons would only let authorized people in and out."

"He'd been killed by his father a few days before Artemis brought you to the Underworld."

"His own father?"

"Yes. Zeus accused Hermes of being a rebel sympathizer and decapitated him before the entire court."

"How horrible!"

"When Hermes's soul arrived in Tartarus, Hades suspected him of being a spy for the loyalists. But one of the Furies overhead him talking with Phobos. Meg—the Fury—was convinced that Hermes truly wanted the two sides to work together. She reported this to Hades, who then convinced Hermes to rescue you."

"I still don't get how Hermes did it, though. How did he break in?"

"He didn't have to. His body was already on Mount Olympus. The gates can't prevent a soul from returning to its body."

"But what about the helm? His soul couldn't wear it, could it?"

Deimos shook his head. "But Hades gave Hermes the power to conjure it."

"How?"

"A god can only conjure a weapon that belongs to him."

Ellie covered her mouth. "Are you saying Hades gave Hermes the helm?"

Deimos nodded. "Of course, Hades expects Hermes to give it back at some point, but it was risky. Hades was unable to make Hermes swear to give it back, because to do so would make the helm a loan and not a gift. It has to belong to the god for the god to conjure it."

"Hermes could have taken advantage of the situation and taken the helm to his father, Zeus. Hermes could have ensured a victory for the loyalists."

"It was a huge risk," Deimos agreed. "I don't know if it's one I would have taken."

"Thank the gods it paid off," Ellie said.

"Thank Hermes," Deimos corrected her. "He was the hero of this story."

"What about Hephaestus?" Ellie asked. "When did he convert?"

"He was with Hades from the beginning," Deimos said. "The loyalists still don't suspect him."

Ellie leaned her head on the back of the couch, her neck against Deimos's arm. She rubbed her belly and imagined the twin girls growing inside. "When will this all be over, Deimos? When will the conflict end?"

"Hecate had a vision," Deimos said softly.

Ellie sat up and squared herself to him. "About me? About the prophesy?"

"About your twins."

Thank you for reading my story. If you enjoyed it, please consider leaving a review. Reviews help other readers to find my books, which helps me.

Please enjoy the first chapter of the next book, *Deimos*.

CHAPTER ONE

Hecate's Vision

Ellie lay on the couch in the moon goddess's cave on Mont Forel, fighting tears. Deimos sat beside her, stroking her arm, as she stared into the fire blazing in the hearth. Hecate slept on a couch opposite them, paralyzed from Zeus's lightning bolt. Rhythmic snores echoed throughout the dark cave, but they weren't Hecate's; they came from deeper in the mountain, where Selene's lover slept.

"Only the Fates know for certain what the future holds," Deimos said, trying to reassure her.

But Ellie could not be reassured.

"Hecate said that her visions sometimes change," he added, raking his hand through his vibrant red hair. "Apollo has said the same."

Ellie clutched her belly as tears fell from her eyes. She'd barely had time to process the news that she was having twin girls, much less the vision of doom from Hecate.

"I won't let anything happen to you or the babies," Deimos said. "I promise."

Ellie knew he meant what he said. She also knew it was a promise he couldn't keep.

Zeus and the loyalists had been desperate to imprison Ellie. If they got wind of this new vision, they would never allow the twins to be born.

Before she'd been paralyzed, Hecate had revealed to Deimos and to the other rebels a recurring vision that had plagued her in recent days. In her vision, the gods were gathered in the great hall on Mount Olympus. Ellie was there with her two little girls. Mount Olympus became bathed in darkness. The mountain shook. The gods gasped and glanced around in horror. The floor of the great hall cracked in half and, as the mountain fell—and the temple along with it—many of the gods fell, too. They fell into the crevice and down into the depths of the mountain, where Gaia—Mother Earth—was waiting with her mouth wide open.

Zeus and Hera were among those who fell. Hecate had been unable to identify everyone who was lost or who remained standing on what was left of the rubble of Mount Olympus. However, she did see among the survivors Ellie, Deimos, and one—only one—of Ellie's twins. The other had fallen, along with Phobos, into the deep abyss and had been swallowed by the darkness.

When Ellie had asked if this meant the end was at least a year away, since her babies were *standing* in the vision, Deimos had shaken his head.

"Gods age differently from humans and from one another. Most age quickly in childhood and then, at adolescence, age so slowly that they seem not to age at all."

"What about pregnancy?" she'd asked. "Is it nine months, like it is for mortals?"

"It's different for every goddess."

Ellie had bit her lip until it had bled. "We could have mere *days*. That's what you're saying."

"I'm afraid so."

She had never felt so hopeless, so full of despair. She was the goddess of lost causes, and yet she could do nothing to help herself.

Now, she closed her eyes. The prayers to her from Phobos broke her heart. He prayed: *Please don't do anything stupid that might jeopardize you and the babies. You can be pigheaded, Ellie. You know you can. Just don't forget about me down here, okay? Deimos may be good looking—damned good looking, it's true. But he's too stuffy for you. Professor Deimos doesn't know how to make you laugh—at least, not as well as I do. Oh, gods, maybe he challenges your mind in ways I can't—or won't. Fuck, Ellie. Maybe you're better off with Deimos.*

By the way, tell Deimos that Aphrodite erased Jaquelyn's memory of the time she overheard us talking about the gods. The girl is blissfully ignorant again.

"Ellie?" Deimos asked, his crystal blue eyes full of concern.

"I want to sleep."

He stroked her cheek. "Good. Get some rest."

He leaned over and touched his lips to hers as he tucked a quilt around her.

Ellie didn't care about rest. She only wanted to stop thinking and feeling and hearing the many prayers that came to her from all over the world. There were so many desperate people praying for their lost causes. Businesses were going under, families were getting evicted, and some weren't sure where they'd get their next meal. But what could Ellie do when her own life and the lives of her babies were in danger?

Sleep would be a welcome escape.

Then, for the first time, she heard a prayer from her mother: *Ellie, where are you? It's a week before Christmas, and I ain't heard nothing from you, child. You don't answer your phone. You stopped sending postcards. For all I know you could be dead.*

"My poor Mama," Ellie whispered. "She's worried sick."

"We'll get word to her as soon as we can," Deimos said. "Now stop worrying and get some rest."

Please, Hypnos, she prayed. *Bring me sleep.*

Deimos carefully extricated himself from the couch, where he'd been sitting beside the sleeping Ellie with her legs draped over his lap. He'd watched her sleep for half an hour, praying to all the gods in the rebellion to protect her and the babies. Now, he needed to stretch his legs and to think. He paced before the fire. He felt like a caged animal at the mercy of his captors, even though he was hiding in the cave by choice.

For six weeks, he'd had to endure watching the love of his life with his brother on the west Texas ranch. Although Deimos had taken comfort in Ellie's prayers to him, he'd come to realize something: Ellie would never choose.

It would almost be cruel to make her do so.

He'd wrestled with the idea of letting her go and had even convinced himself that he would—that it was the right thing to do, if he really loved her. But the moment she was in his arms again, he knew he couldn't do it—not to himself or to her. They needed one another. They belonged together.

After holding her in his arms again, he truly believed that, if he walked away to spare her from having to choose, she'd be miserable without him. And he knew the same would be true if she gave up his brother.

Ellie was waiting to let the paternity of her babies decide, but Deimos knew in his heart that it didn't matter—not because he believed in Hecate's vision, but because he believed Ellie would *always* love Phobos as much as she loved him.

When Hecate had shared her vision with the rebellion in the throne room of the Underworld, Artemis had said something to Deimos that had upset him. She'd said, "It looks like you get the girl in the end."

It had taken every bit of his self-control not to berate her. Instead, he'd taken a deep breath and had asked, "Do you really think I'd pay such a price?"

Artemis had glared at him with her forest-green eyes. "Watch your tone! I was only kidding."

"Some gods are more than willing to throw their brothers, sons, and daughters to the wolves," Hades had said. "You can't blame Artemis for believing you to be one of them."

"I was only kidding," Artemis had said again.

Persephone had placed her slender arm around her husband's waist. "Let's get back to the plan, darling. What are we going to do?"

"I've said from the beginning—when Apollo first brought this talk of a reckoning to our attention—that we gods are being judged. If we want to come out of this unscathed, we must, no matter how bad things get, take the high moral ground."

Deimos had found those words to be ironic, considering that Hades had once been accused of attempting to kill one of his children while it was still in the womb, but Deimos had held his tongue.

Artemis had raised her bow. "We protect Ellie."

"And her babies," Hermes had added.

"At all cost," Hephaestus had said.

Hypnos and Thanatos had agreed.

"I believe that's the only hope we have of saving ourselves," Hades had said.

For the members of the rebellion, saving Ellie and her babies meant saving themselves; for Deimos, it was about love. It wasn't the arrow of love or the arrow of hate driving him; the two arrows had canceled each other out. This was his *heart*, which had come to care for another more than he'd ever thought possible. He would fight to protect Ellie from Zeus and the loyalists, and, if Hecate's vision came to be, he would do everything in his power to save his brother and Ellie's child—a child that he felt, deep in his soul, belonged to him, too.

Ellie stirred. When her eyes sought his across the room, Deimos grinned. She returned his smile, filling his heart with everything good. Her smile vanquished the anxiety that had taken over his thoughts. He flew to her and knelt by her side.

"I was dreaming about you," she whispered.

"A good dream, I hope."

"*Very* good."

"Thank you, Hypnos."

"Can I have a kiss?"

Deimos cradled her head and brought her mouth to his. He closed his eyes and breathed in her scent, licked her lips to enjoy her taste. Then he caressed her cheek before sliding his hand to her throat, her chest. Her heart pounded beneath his fingertips as he deepened his kiss and cupped her breast.

"Oh, Deimos," she whispered against his lips.

"I want you so badly," he whispered back.

"You can have me," she said.

Deimos glanced over at Hecate, who was still sleeping, before he tugged off his shirt and helped Ellie out of hers. They scrambled from their shoes and pants before he climbed beside her on the couch, his chest against her breasts. With his hands on her lower back, he pressed her against him. She rubbed herself against his thigh, sending shocks of desire through every muscle in his body. His hands sought her bottom before he whipped her around, putting himself beneath her. She sat up and straddled him, with her knees on either side of him. Her breasts dangled over him as she lifted her bottom and found him waiting for that hot, moist spot. She guided him and moaned with pleasure as he entered.

Deimos tried to be quiet, so as not to wake the others sleeping in the cave, but his efforts were in vain. The intense pleasure he felt, as Ellie raised and lowered herself, found a way to his throat, and he gasped and moaned until he exploded with ecstasy.

Ellie collapsed against him. He smoothed her hair and kissed her shoulder.

As much as he wanted to lie there, skin against skin, for however long they wished, Deimos knew Selene would soon return. He sat up and held Ellie on his lap as he kissed her once more. Then he said, "We better get dressed."

"Don't do it on my account," Selene said from the entrance to her cave, her luminous long hair and robe billowing in the breeze. She sat in her chariot, smirking.

"Selene!" Deimos pulled the quilt from the floor and wrapped it around Ellie, while he used his powers to instantly dress them. "I didn't hear you arrive."

"Obviously." She climbed from the chariot and unbridled her horses. "But don't mind me. I'm going to bed. Maybe I'll make love to Endymion first, now that you've got me in the mood."

Ellie climbed from Deimos's lap and sat beside him with crimson cheeks.

"I thought you said that your wards are weakest on the new moon, while you sleep," Deimos pointed out. "Should I stand guard?"

"No," she said. "I put up extra protections yesterday. No one will get past them."

Just then Hermes appeared, holding the helm of invisibility. "I wouldn't go so far as to say *that*."

"Hermes!" Deimos gawked. "How long have you been there beneath the helm?"

Hermes's cheeks turned nearly as red as Ellie's. "Er, not long."

Deimos glanced at Ellie who wouldn't meet his eyes. She curled the quilt around her and stared at the fire in the hearth.

It was one thing to know that gods could see through clothes and buildings and so forth, but it was another to know that they'd been right there in the room with you during your most vulnerable moment.

"Why have you come?" Selene asked.

Hermes wore a scabbard and shield that Deimos had never seen before. "Well, you see, I went to return the helm to Lord Hades, and he told me to deliver it to Ellie."

Ellie looked up at Hermes with wide eyes. "To me? Why?"

"He knew you'd return to Phobos."

Deimos jumped to his feet. "Even with the helm, that would be risky."

Hermes handed the helm to Ellie. "True. But now you have options."

"Thank you," Ellie said.

Hermes removed the scabbard and shield and handed them to Ellie. "Hephaestus made these for you. Deimos can show you how to use and to conjure them."

"To what?" Ellie looked up at Deimos. She had the weapons draped across the quilt on her lap.

"I'll explain later," Deimos assured her. Then, he asked Hermes, "Any updates?"

"I'm going to bed," Selene said. "You can catch me up later." Then, to her horses, she said, "Come on, ladies. To your stalls."

Selene flew to the back of the cave, where her lover was sleeping. Her mares followed.

"Not much to report," Hermes said as he scratched his curly black head. "Hephaestus is still working on Athena. I expect they'll set up a meeting with her soon."

Deimos gnawed on his lower lip. Athena was unpredictable. He feared approaching her would backfire.

Hermes crossed the room to where Hecate lay. He touched her cheek.

She opened her eyes and smiled up at him. Her black and white hair lay in long strands across her pillow.

"You can move your mouth," Hermes said. "That's progress."

"I'm thirsty," she said.

Hermes found a goblet on the table beside the couch and gently lifted Hecate's head while she drank.

"Thank you," she said when she'd finished.

"How do you feel?" Hermes asked.

"Stiff."

Hermes took a seat on the couch with Hecate's feet in his lap. "Maybe if we get your blood flowing." He massaged her stockinged feet.

"I wish I could feel that," Hecate said.

"You'll be good as new before long, Hecate." Deimos returned to his seat beside Ellie.

"Are *you* having visions now?" she teased.

"I wish," Deimos said with a laugh.

"No, you don't," Hecate said. "I wouldn't wish them on anyone. It's a curse, especially when there's rarely anything to be done about them."

"You said there's a chance," Deimos said, not wanting to add to Ellie's despair.

"There's always a chance," she said. "However slight."

"When can we get a message to Phobos?" Ellie asked. "I can't imagine how hard it must be on him, to not know what's going on."

"I'd like to watch over Hecate while you're gone," Hermes said. "Assuming you're going with her, Deimos."

Deimos gaped for a moment. "Uh, we can't go *now*. Ellie doesn't know how to use her powers. She needs some training before we attempt something that dangerous."

"Agreed," Hermes said. "Summon me when you're ready."

Hermes vanished.

Ellie pulled her sword from its jeweled scabbard. "Are you really going to teach me how to use these things?"

"Of course," he said. "You have a lot to learn, so we better get started."

EVA POHLER

Eva Pohler is a *USA Today* bestselling author of over thirty novels in multiple genres, including mysteries, thrillers, and young adult paranormal romance based on Greek mythology. Her books have been described as "addictive" and "sure to thrill"—*Kirkus Reviews*.

To learn more about Eva and her books, and to sign up to hear about new releases, and sales, please visit her website at www.evapohler.com.